Men of the Wise Oak

Men of the Wise Oak

by

Oliver J Tooley

Copyright 2020 © Oliver J. Tooley

The right of Oliver J. Tooley to be identified as the author of this work has been asserted. All rights reserved. No unauthorised copying of any part of this book permitted.

Edited by Sarah Dawes

Cover design Oliver J. Tooley

Blue Poppy Publishing 2020

ISBN: 9-798-602690-73-6

Oliver J. Tooley

Dedicated to anyone who waited
nearly three years for this.

Sorry

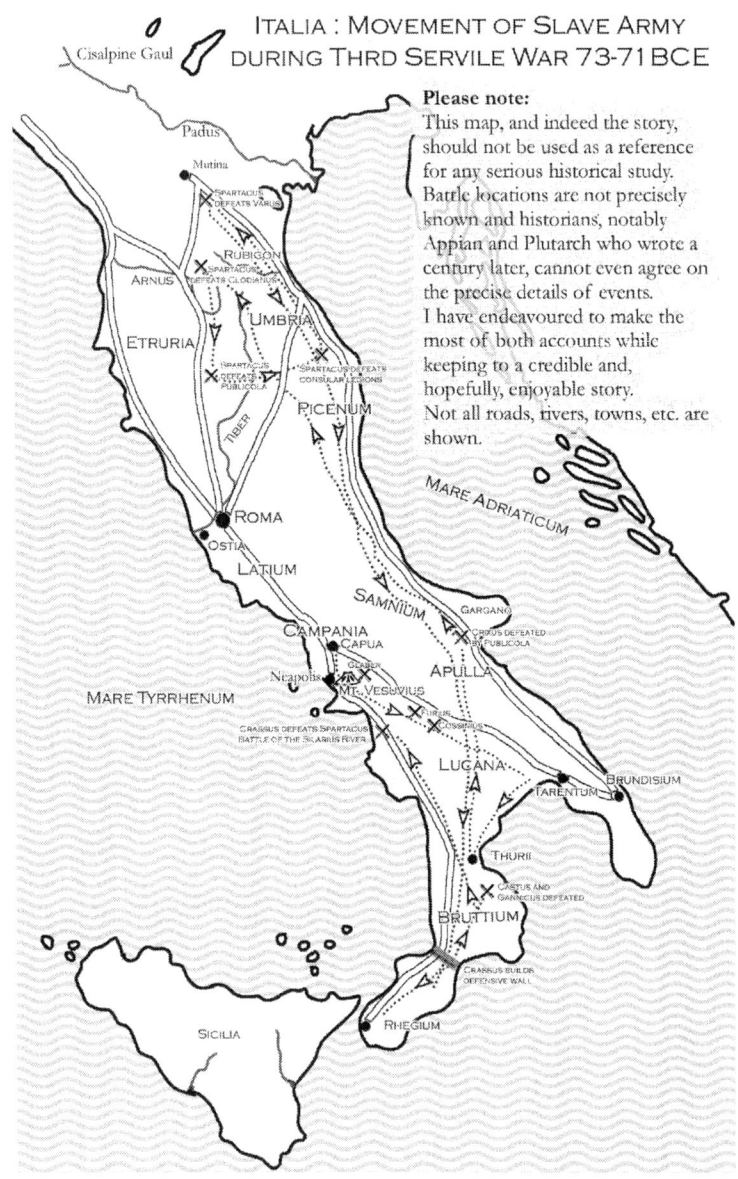

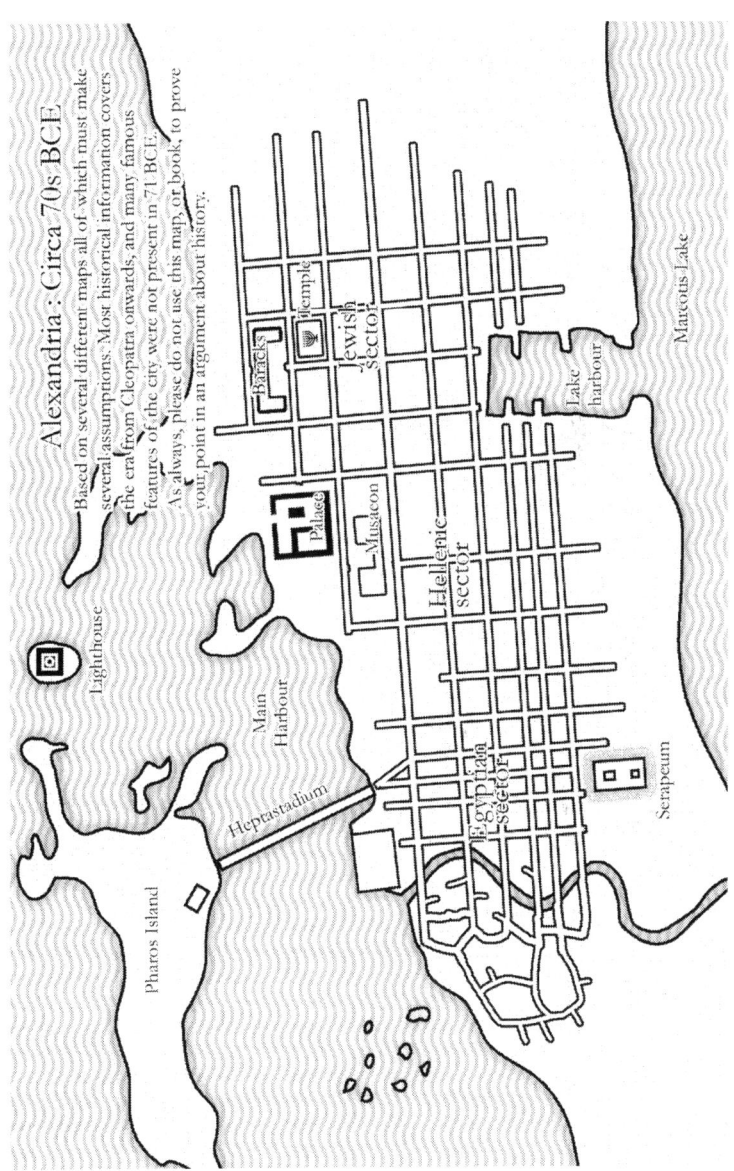

1

Wind seethed over the sweeping desolate landscape as though the searing white snowfields, broken by dark rocky outcrops, with occasional battered and cowering conifers, had offended the Gods themselves.

A lone figure, dark against the snow, trudged purposefully onwards. Tall and slim, he was cloaked in blue and carrying a staff topped with a polished stone which reflected the sunlight. Blyth was young and in love, and the object of his affection, Blodwyth, had been kidnapped by raiders from the north, from the peaceful island where they were both training to become Deru-Weidi. The mages of the oak-groves taught selected young Keltoi for twenty years. They were expected to learn everything: the poems and songs, the creation stories and legends, the histories of their tribes, the names and domains of the many Gods and Goddesses that ruled over every aspect of life, and the sacred laws that governed the people. Even the chiefs and high chiefs of the tribes took their lead from the law and the mages.

They were also taught the laws of nature. Understanding the medicinal effects of plant extracts, and human anatomy, made them effective physicians on the battlefield or in the village. Other secret scientific knowledge allowed them to appear magical to the farmers and warriors who revered them. A few of those selected were also possessed of genuine magical powers. Blyth was one of those few.

At twenty-six years of age, after less than ten years of formal training combined with much painful experience gathered as a result of his fiery temper, his full powers were as yet unknown, unproven. Yet there were those who suspected Blyth could be more powerful even than his great-grandfather, Kaito, the oldest and wisest of the Deru-Weidi. Only time would tell - time, and the nature of the challenges that the Gods presented to him. But now his mind was focussed, in a very literal sense, on finding Blodwyth and bringing her home safely. The previous summer he had invoked ancient magic to bond her to him by blood. They were blood kin; Blodwyth's blood ran through his veins, and his through hers. In an indefinable way, he knew that she was alive, and he could feel the right way to go, although not precisely how far.

In the distance he could see smoke, but no habitation as yet. Somewhere ahead there had to be a village or, at the very least, a camp. Earlier he had passed a shelter that appeared abandoned yet, on investigation, was clearly built to last. Low circular walls had been constructed with flat stones, painstakingly selected for the way they fitted together, using the barest scraps of soil for mortar. The roof was grown over with grasses, now with a covering of snow. Inside, through a heavy wooden door in the small opening, steps led down to the dug-out floor. Here, Blyth could see, larger stones spanned the roof; so large that many people would have had to work together with considerable organisation to lift them into place. There was nothing else here: no food stores, no tools, no furniture or other evidence of habitation. The central fire was long dead although the floor was clearly blackened, and the remains of the last fire lay undisturbed in this windless haven. Blyth concluded, wrongly, that the house had been built and then abandoned by a family who had simply moved on.

He felt, with the tendrils of his mind, for Blodwyth, sensing he was closer. Could he reach the village where the smoke was coming from before nightfall? Probably not. He had a good cloak and plenty of food. Lighting a fire was as easy as pointing his staff at the fuel, nevertheless the sky was clear, which meant a cold night. Even when Bellenos, the sun god, had reached the highest point in the sky he was still noticeably to the south. He would be disappearing soon, and the new day would begin at sunset, just as the world had begun with darkness, before the sun god was created. With no cloud cover the temperature would drop rapidly, but the wind was the greater challenge. It was unrelenting, driving the fallen snow before it, scouring the landscape. Blyth imagined he would wake up and find he had been completely covered in snowdrifts. If he woke up at all. Resigned to returning to the abandoned house, he turned around and retraced his steps, eagerly anticipating relief from the incessant wind.

2

In the first pale light before dawn, Epona's eyes flickered open. Moving quietly to avoid disturbing anyone else, she felt for her staff which had been beside her as she slept. It wasn't there. She looked to find it and Kaito handed her a morning drink without a word. He glanced to where her staff leaned against the wall of the roundhouse.

Epona sighed deeply and took a sip of the infusion.

"Go on," she said, "I know what you're going to say, and you are not going to convince me."

"Then there seems no point in saying it." Kaito gave her an enigmatic look.

"He's my son!"

"He's my great-grandson. What relevance does any of this have?"

"I have to find him."

"He has to find himself." Kaito was almost irritatingly calm.

"I told you, you can't change my mind."

"He won't thank you."

Epona sipped her drink. It was both soothing and invigorating at once.

"I don't need his thanks. I need him alive."

Kaito left a long pause while he too sipped the hot liquid in his own cup. Then he said, "He isn't Trethiwr you know."

"What is that supposed to mean?" Epona shot him a look.

"You know very well."

"I know he is not Trethiwr, but he is very like him."

"And Trethiwr would have wanted you chasing after him on his journeys across the world?"

"Of course he wouldn't. He was a man; and a mage of immense power."

"As is Blyth, on both counts. If he were a warrior, would you follow him into the battle and hold a shield over him? If he were a farmer, would you plough his field and chase off the wolves from the herd? If he were a craftsman would you sharpen his tools, or blow his furnace? He is a Deru-Weido and he has chosen a path to follow."

Epona appeared to deflate at this.

Kaito went on, "You haven't seen Blyth for some years, but he was already a man when you last saw him. From what I understand, he may surpass his father, and even perhaps me, in his magical ability before he is through. The Gods have seen fit to give our family a natural ability to control the elements but alas, in their capriciousness, they haven't always given us the wisdom to wield it for the best outcome. Nevertheless, if you go chasing after him he will not be grateful. The time has come to let him go. There is nothing more they can teach him at Lugh-Dun or Ynys-Mona and, as for your fears for his safety, you should fear more for those who cross him. Besides, I have other work for you if you will accept it."

"What would you have me do?"

"Gwenn has been freed from her bondage to the Roman patrician, but she is still not free of him."

Epona interrupted, "Argh, not that stinking pestilential city again!"

"Is it really so awful? I only went there once and stayed outside the city, at the home of an important senator. It seemed a remarkable place."

"It is a pit of vermin and stinks like an old latrine. And the arrogance of the people! Argh, you would think they had created the world itself."

"The Romani do have a strong sense of self-belief, yes. In one sense, it is their blessing; nobody ever did anything truly wonderful without first having a belief in themselves and their abilities. It permeates every moment of their waking lives, from the moment of birth, to their last gasping breath and, while they live, they demand much of themselves in order to live up to their own shining image. Yet perhaps it may also become their downfall. For, just as their pride drives their achievements, it may yet allow them to become complacent, and when a man is overcome with pride and complacency, he can be destroyed simply because he cannot imagine the method that might bring about his downfall."

Kaito had been almost talking to himself, as much as to Epona. She waited, not sure what to say next. Eventually, he came out of his reverie and appeared to remember that Epona was there.

He went on, "Anyway, you don't have to go anywhere near Rome this time. She has gone to Campania, in search of her friend and contact. His name is Titus, and his ancestors were from Galatia. I believe Gwenn is still emotionally enslaved to the Roman, Gaius Julius Caesar, even though he has freed her from legal slavery. I don't know what will break that bond, but she may not be irrevocably lost to our cause. I want you to find her and see what you can discover."

Epona sighed, "If you really think it will do any good, Kaito, I will go to Campania."

"I thank you for your loyalty, Epona."

At this point Teague had awoken.

"Will you be going after Blyth, Mater?"

"Not for now. Kaito persuaded me that Blyth may yet be a match for the difficulties he will face, and he has another job for me."

Kaito added, "You two young men need to go back to finish your studies, and I think it is high time Elarch joined you at Ynys-Mona. I will take you. It has been too long since I saw Llwyd and Alisa."

Epona looked surprised, "She is approaching her nineteenth summer, is she not?" Even as she said this she felt a stab of realisation at how old she herself had become. The last of her babies was now a mature woman. She also felt a stab of guilt; how had she neglected to teach Elarch about the ways of the Deru-Weidi? She went on, "Isn't Elarch too old to begin training as a Deru-Weida?"

Kaito gave her an enigmatic look, "Who said anything about beginning?"

3

Blyth lit a fire in the hut. The flickering light and smoke filled the darkness inside, while outside the sky blackened and the wind whipped the snow into drifts against the walls. He wrapped his heavy woollen cloak, reeking of sheep, around him, and closed his eyes.

Blyth couldn't remember falling asleep, but he woke to the sound of voices just outside and then the door opened and in stepped two bulky men in heavy cloaks. The fire was burning lower, so he must have been asleep for a fair while, but the presence of the strangers had the effect of a bucket of cold water in the face and he scrambled to his feet, with staff in hand; prepared. He could feel his heart beating, like an army beating their shields before battle. His heart was preparing for battle.

The men had the warning of a lit fire but no knowledge of who was in the house, so they were on their guard. The first man filled the doorway, sword drawn, shield in hand. When he spoke, the sounds that emerged were largely unintelligible to Blyth. Big hairy dogs strained on ropes held by the second man, behind the first, their teeth reflecting the ember glow of the fire.

Blyth was trapped. With seemingly no words in common he could not communicate except by gestures. He could of course summon up enough magic to destroy them but so far, they had not done anything to deserve such a fate, besides, should this come to a fight, there would be no time for Blyth to check the strength of any spell he used. He might blow the entire hut to the four winds, taking him and the strangers and their dogs with it. There was room to stand, and room perhaps for the swordsman to take two paces to the centre and touch the walls with his sword in any direction. Switching the staff to his left hand he opened his right palm outwards facing them, showing he held no weapon, and smiled his most winning smile.

"Blyth," he said simply, touching his chest with his right hand.

The swordsman relaxed, imperceptibly, but kept his weapon drawn. Blyth was never comfortable looking straight into another man's eyes. Instead his gaze followed the rounded tip of the big iron sword. It was a slashing weapon of course, useless for stabbing. The stranger no doubt had spears, which he might have left outside when he came in to investigate.

It occurred to Blyth that, just as he could have killed the men by now, so too could they have tried to kill him. If they wanted to fight first and talk later, they would have set the dogs on him. Slowly he laid down his staff. Then he moved slowly towards his pack, keeping his eyes on the sword, and his hands open and in view. He lifted the flap over the bag with fingertips and located a strip of meat which he offered to the swordsman. He would have to put down either the sword or the shield to accept the gift. The decision seemed to cost him all his mental effort, but eventually he slung the shield on his back, and sheathed the sword. A double result.

As he took the meat and passed some to his partner the dogs took the opportunity to break free from their master's grasp. The two canines barged past the swordsman and in a single bound were on Blyth. A low guttural sound emerged from deep in his throat, his eyes changed colour from brown to amber, and both dogs fell back in confusion, rolling on the floor and scampering away, tails between legs. As the swordsman reached again for his blade. Blyth moved towards the nearest dog and uttered a soothing sound, the dog came to him, meekly, letting Blyth pet him behind the ears. The second dog rolled over in front of Blyth, legs in the air, while the strangers gaped, open mouthed.

Blyth, grinning, kept his eyes on the men and gestured as he said, "Dogs, Blyth, friends," grasping his own wrists with his hands mimicking a greeting.

He smiled at the men and added "You, Blyth, friends?" repeating the gesture.

His heart was still battering down the walls of his chest, but it looked as though the immediate danger had passed.

The swordsman held out his hands, palms open and facing Blyth, then offered his right hand. Blyth grasped the man's wrist, and he Blyth's. Then the ritual of greeting was performed between Blyth and the dog handler.

Once again, Blyth touched his chest and said, "Blyth."

The men responded in turn with their names, Gharath ab Nechtan, and Uthrien ab Duberr. Blyth followed their cue, adding his patronymic, "Blyth ab Trethiwr." He felt a lump in his throat from saying his father's name like that.

It turned out that they had many words in common, although even those were dialectally different. The men were traders regularly travelling south to trade with the Brigantii, and so gradually all three found it easiest to speak in that dialect. Gharath and Uthrien explained how they had been delayed but had been aiming to reach this hut before sunset. Blyth apologised, explaining that he too had been caught out by the short day and that he had presumed the hut to be abandoned. As they all sat round Blyth's fire, now roaring again, they told him they were glad they did not have to light a fire after such an arduous day and the three shared out the food they had remaining. Blyth thought for a while about how tense it had been only a short while earlier, and how relaxed everything was now. How, if things had gone even slightly differently, either he, or the traders might now be dead, or forced to continue a journey in the windswept snowy night. Yet still even now, he sensed there was an uneasy truce between them. They had shaken hands, and shared bread, but none really wanted to be the first to sleep.

They sat around the fire telling stories, heads drooping, the dogs snuggled either side of Blyth. Little sparks spun and danced in the heat eddies above the fluttering flames. Gharath passed a small wine skin round; the liquid was fiery and warming. Blyth only took a small sip. He felt the spirit warm him from within, but he knew too much would reverse the effect.

4

Blyth woke and gradually remembered where he was. His hand stroked warm fur, the air smelled of dogs, wood smoke, alcohol and body sweat. Alarmed, he realised he had fallen asleep. The two traders were already awake and had set water to heat over the fire. They hadn't killed him then, Blyth mused. He smiled inwardly at the strange, dark, humour of that thought; if they had, he would hardly be thinking about it. He thought about how mistrust of strangers has more to do with ignorance than knowledge. Once you know someone, you find out they are just like you. It had been the same when he was in Rome. He had met a young Roman patrician the same age as him - exactly the same age if their calculations between different calendars had been correct - and despite the fact that they were from completely different cultures, should indeed have been implacable enemies, they had more in common than they had differences.

Uthrien passed a cup to Blyth. The infusion was weak but hot and Blyth drank it as quickly has he could bear to get the warmth inside him. There was no more food in his pack.

"Can we reach the next village in daylight?"

"If we get going quickly and make good progress."

Uthrien hefted his pack onto his back and called the dogs.

"Are you coming?"

By way of an answer, Blyth scrambled to his feet, grabbed his pack and staff and adjusted his cloak.

The wind had died, the rising sun was still low on the horizon, and the landscape a brilliant unbroken white in every direction. Their breath wreathed in coils of vapour in the eerie silence. The men hitched the dogs to small sleds, laden with bundles of furs and other goods. The dogs pulled from the front, while the men pushed from behind. They set a fast pace, but Blyth didn't mind as it helped keep him warm in the freezing air. Long before the sun reached its highest point the hut behind them had blended imperceptibly into the blank landscape.

To their left, in the distance, a forest stretched away up the slope towards the further steep mountains. A herd of red deer pawed at the snow-covered ground, close to the edge of the forest, where the trees were less dense, cropping the sparse grass and heather or scraping mosses and lichens from the gaunt trees.

Blyth indicated the herd with a signal suggesting they hunt. Gharath eyed up the herd. The nearest animal was three spear throws distant and closer than that to the cover of the trees. He swept his hand across in the gesture that meant 'no hunt'. Blyth thought about the way hunting signals seemed much more universal than spoken language. Were they innate, or a gift from the Gods?

Blyth tried again; he gave the signal to hunt and pointed out a young male slightly detached from the main herd. It had wandered off to the right where another small stand of low shrubs offered him the promise of some early shoots and perhaps longer grass. It was further away from the main forest, but also further from the hunters. Gharath looked uncertain, Uthrien appeared willing to give it a go. They spoke softly in their own language, Blyth understood enough to know Gharath had persuaded Uthrien to wait until they reached the village. They turned back to the sleds, but Blyth blocked their path. It took a lot for him to look Gharath directly into his eyes but he did so now and made the signal to hunt with as much emphasis as he could, once again identifying the prey, the young buck furthest from the herd. Gharath turned his head to the side with a curious expression and looked over at the buck. They would struggle to make the village before sunset if they stopped to hunt now, and he knew they had next to no chance of making a kill. The herd would spook the moment the men began to move towards them. They had only remained calm thus far because the hunters were too far away to be a threat. Blyth turned with a deliberate look and smoothly lifted his staff to point it at the selected buck. He began to walk towards the herd. He hadn't gone very far when, as expected, the more alert animals began to move slowly towards the safety of the forest, calling in alarm to the others who soon caught on. Only the buck remained unmoved. Blyth kept his staff pointed at it, as he continued on, moving towards a point halfway between the buck and the rest of the herd. He signalled to Gharath and Uthrien to move in quickly. Uthrien drew his sling, and selected a good-sized stone, Gharath hefted a throwing spear. Although the sling had a longer range, the spear was more certain. Blyth was drawing in now from the left, Gharath directly from the front, and Uthrien was sweeping round to the right. But their manoeuvring, although as natural as breathing to them, was unnecessary. The buck remained motionless, even as they drew within spear throwing range. Uthrien signalled to Gharath to take the shot when he was ready. It was all over in a few minutes. The spell was broken when the spear struck but, with so much time to prepare, and a standing target, it was a kill-shot.

The traders eyed Blyth warily, with a strange mixture of emotions, as he trussed the deer onto a hastily prepared pole frame and began dragging the heavy carcass through the snow towards the village without another word.

5

Passing through the lands of the Deceangli was a risky business for most travellers. Their warriors were traditional in their love of raiding for cattle and sheep, and for taking hostages to ransom, although they would never attack Deru-Weidi. There were, however, others, who were outcast by the Deru-Weidi. These bandits were no longer part of society, no longer protected by the law, with no hope of entering the halls of Lugh after death. In winter, with the ground hard, a traveller did not have to keep to the high road. Indeed, with the mountain slopes covered in snow, it was safer on lower ground, and warmer, out of the wind, on the forest paths. But that left the unwary traveller open to banditry. Kaito knew they had nothing to fear, but he suspected that a small band of spearmen had been following them for some time. He hoped they knew who, and indeed what, he was. He rode a black stallion. Elarch, Teague, and Abbon rode alongside. The horses were nervous, which only served to reinforce Kaito's feeling that there was some hidden danger among the trees. Kaito's blue cloak set him apart and clearly identified him as a mage. His companions wore cloaks woven in the pattern of the Dwr-y-tryges, which also clearly marked them out as outsiders here. They gave the outward impression of an easy target. Kaito thought, 'If they would attack a mage, better that they attack me. If there were bandits who would attack a Deru-Weido, then far better one who could protect himself easily and teach them a lesson never to forget'. As long as he could keep Elarch safe. He knew both Abbon and Teague could take care of themselves if there was any trouble.

Gaunt skeletons of oak, ash, beech and birch mingled with conifers bristling with dark green needles. Ivy scrambled up the trunks, seeking a slow sinister strangulation. There would be mistletoe as well, higher up in the tallest branches. Holly grew at regular intervals, the area around them cleared allowing them to grow tall, well above the height of a man. The lower leaves were glossy and spiny against the attentions of all but the hardiest herbivores, their red berries poisonous to all but a handful of birds. High up in the holly branches, the leaves were oval, lacking any spikes. These were maintained with great care by the herdsmen because they were a vital source of animal feed in the worst of the winter.

Elarch noticed the holly leaves. She had not seen this before since her village was much further south and, although the winters were harsh, there was usually enough fodder to keep the bulk of the herd through until Imbolc. Kaito realised that he had not got around to telling her the story of how the holly had come to be like this, and so he told her now, although both her brothers would know the story already.

"As you already know, way back in the time of the first men, there was no winter. The sun shone, and the rains kept the soil wet. Food grew in abundance in fields and woodlands. But those early men were greedy and demanded more from the Gods. Offended, the Gods destroyed all the people, sparing only one man, Iuestos, and his family. Iuestos repopulated the world but, as a warning to men not to be too greedy, the sun god Bellenos deserted them for half of every year.

"Epona and Cernunnos were forced to desert the people too; because without the sun they could not make the crops grow or the forests abundant. But Cernunnos took pity on the men, who were beset by the north winds while the ground was buried under deep snows. He saw their cattle and sheep grow thin, unable to find food before Imbolc. So, he found a small holly bush, whose leaves remained green and fresh all winter, and he cut off the spines making the leaves smooth. He showed the men how their sheep and cattle and other livestock could eat these leaves and stay healthy all winter, but when the men were away, wild animals came and ate the leaves and the holly died.

"So Cernunnos found another holly bush and made it grow as tall as an oak tree. He reached up and cut off all the spines on the leaves, above the height of a tall man's reach. Then he showed the men how they could cut the branches down and feed their livestock even in the worst depths of winter. From that time until this, when any holly is allowed to grow taller than a man's reach, the leaves above that height are always smooth edged and can be cut down to feed the livestock, but they are too high for wild animals to steal them."

They rode on in silence for a while, as Elarch thought about this story, and Kaito was lost in his own thoughts, when two spearmen rushed from the trees in front of him, yelling loudly. Several more emerged on both sides. Kaito's mount remained still, under his control, Teague and Abbon urged their horses into a gallop and burst through the undergrowth out of the trap. Elarch's grey mare was spooked. It reared up, Elarch just clinging on, before cantering a short distance away. She was quickly captured by other warriors, revealing themselves from behind trees, armed with ropes.

Kaito was surrounded, as the men came close enough to plunge their spears into him, but he remained calm. The men would want to capture them alive, and not seriously hurt, if they were to hold them to ransom. Ropes were thrown over his horse's head and pulled tight and another man tried to drag him from the saddle. As soon as he grabbed at the fine blue linen cloak the raider flew backwards as though he had been kicked by the horse. The others looked startled but did not yet assume the blow had been struck by this small wiry old man, on the fine horse. How could it have been? Whoever he was, he would fetch a high price once they found out his tribe. He was unarmed and dressed in fine clothes. They assumed that the two young men who had fled had been the guard, although they appeared to be unarmed as well.

Some of the men who had captured Elarch had already pulled her from her mount and were dragging her away. She looked back at Kaito who was fully occupied with men surrounding him and hauling on the ropes around his horse's neck. The men who now had Elarch's grey mare began to examine the contents of the packs and found many herbs and potions. Glancing back at their comrades-in-arms trying to wrest the black stallion from the rider, they saw another man thrown backwards through the air like chaff in the wind. The smartest among them began to realise that something was not right here, and he quickly mounted the mare and tried to ride her away from the scene. The horse, however, was not easily biddable. She reared and bucked like a wild thing. The thief held on for some time, then Abbon dropped from the trees above and knocked him off the horse. Meanwhile every man who had attempted to attack Kaito had found themselves thrown violently away. The men who were abducting Elarch were suddenly attacked by a wildcat, which leapt from the undergrowth.

Gradually it began to dawn on the few remaining attackers that they had made a terrible mistake. They backed away hurriedly and fled. This left the challenge of rescuing Elarch, who was now out of sight, having been dragged into the dense woodland by her captors. Kaito focused his mind on her. Abbon and Teague came to join him, but before they could go to her rescue, there was shouting out of sight in the trees, and the sound of animals in panic. Elarch emerged seemingly placid and unscathed. Kaito said nothing, keeping his thoughts to himself.

All the attackers had fled, except one young man of perhaps fourteen summers. He had barely been involved in the attack at all. He appeared transfixed, rooted to the spot, amazed at the events which had unfolded, yet the look on his face, as he stared at Kaito, Teague, Abbon, and Elarch, was not fear, but wonder.

6

Epona stood in the prow of the ship and gazed at the unbroken blue sky reflected in the soothing muscular waves of the sea. Her copper hair tied in complex plaits glinted in the sunlight. The leather sails cracked in the breeze while the single row of oarsmen on each side dipped the tips of their oars in unison, breaking the polished bulging surface of the water in little white foamy crests. This was her fiftieth summer, by her reckoning. By that age, an ordinary woman could look forward to being an old-mother, revered and respected by the village folk, their views sought on matters of concern. Few women even reached that age, and even fewer men. She would be honoured in their village when she had grandchildren, and perhaps even great-grandchildren, running around. Epona was different though. She was a Deru-Weida. The Deru-Weidi were honoured already, from the moment they ceased being acolytes they would take on the role of mage adviser in one village or another, their words the words of the Gods, translated for the chiefs and kings.

But Epona was blessed with magical powers. She would live longer than ordinary people if she was not killed in some misadventure. She did not feel the ravages of old age, as any normal woman beginning her sixth decade beyond the halls of Lugh would do. In fact, she felt vibrant, more alive than she had in some time. But at the back of her mind there was a nagging worry. Her husband was dead, and she had done nothing to help him.

He had sent her away, for her safety; and she had gone, taking her daughter Elarch with her. She should have known that something terrible was going to happen. While she was gone, Trethiwr had angered the village mage. He had allowed the villagers to take him and kill him, even though he could have blown them apart with a thought. So why did she feel guilty? It was obvious he had wanted to die and had chosen the method and time of his death. What she didn't know was why. Other than the fact that she knew the Gods had made plans for him, that he had been both blessed and cursed by them for their own unfathomable reasons. If she had been there, could she have helped him? Could she have soothed his broken soul? Talked him out of it, or fought off his tormentors until he felt able to cope with life again? Would he even have thanked her if she had? She could never know, but she knew she would wonder until they met again at Lugh's feasting table, and shared mead and stories around the fire.

She turned away from the endless sea and went back to where the captain stood in the centre, with his keen eyes on everything.

"Do you expect a smooth crossing?" she asked, by way of conversation.

"You should know more than anyone, Deru-Weida. Have you not read the omens?"

"I've yet to meet a sailor who didn't know more about the future just by observing the clouds, the direction of the winds, the colour of the sunrise and sunset, and the movements of birds than any number of Deru-Weidi casting over the guts of a sheep. But the signs were good enough that I sought passage with you, if that puts you at ease."

"What you say may be true, but the Goddess is a fickle mistress. She protects us when it is her whim and takes us when the fancy takes her. I expect a calm crossing; with this breeze in the sails, and the oarsmen, we should make land by tomorrow morning.

Few ships ventured beyond the sight of land in winter. The seas could change without warning, winds could drop off or change direction. Or worse, a storm could whip up waves twice the height of the sails, rain lashing down hard enough to fill the deck with water, and the threat of Taranis striking the mast with a thunderbolt. The Goddess of the seas was among the more capricious of all the Gods, and she was without mercy when she took men to her.

Despite this, Gallic fishermen and traders still made the short crossing between the island of Pretan, which the Greeks called Albion, and the Romans called Britannia, to the northern shores of Gaul, or Gallia as the

Romans called it. From there Epona would face a long and tedious journey across Gaul and into Italia by land because in winter almost nobody sailed on the middle sea, even though it was calmer than the waters around Pretan. The Romani were not natural sailors, and they would not venture out except when conditions were perfect. So Epona resigned herself to the thought of travelling through the Roman territories of Gallia Narbonensis and all the way down the coast roads, past Rome itself, until she reached Campania where she hoped to catch up with Gwenn and try to persuade her to come home. She didn't know which she dreaded more; losing her old friend or having to tolerate the Romans' peculiar sanitary arrangements.

7

Gharath was speaking to a man who Blyth had to assume was the chief. He had not picked up enough of the language to make out much more than some sort of honorific applied to the chief, his own name being repeated, and the names of some tribes including his own.

The chief did not manage to compose his features into anything resembling pleasure during the entire speech. He sat, brooding like a thundercloud, the firelight reflected off the torcs on his neck and arms. 'Silver,' Blyth thought, 'not gold. Perhaps they have no gold, or perhaps there is a bigger chief in another more powerful village to whom he pays homage.' Next to the chief another man stood looking even more sour faced. His ornate cloak, the only one with any ornamentation among the entourage, picked him out as someone very important. A mage, Blyth guessed.

In the reddish light the man's cloak looked almost black, but Blyth thought it was probably blue. He pondered, 'Woad surely does not grow in such a cold land as this, so it must have been imported at great expense.

The bright coloured threads, used to embroider the fabric in intricate patterns, must surely have cost more than the cloak itself.' They shone out, in yellow, red, and silver, detailing two circles joined by a line, with another line bisecting that, and then angled off in opposite directions, like a stylised bolt of lightning. The symbolism was unknown to Blyth, he guessed at the sun and moon, and perhaps it was intended to be lightning.

His thoughts were interrupted. The chief was speaking to him and the tone of voice told Blyth he was not pleased. Gharath told him to kneel. Before Blyth had given it any thought he dropped down onto one knee, placing his staff on the floor, and bowed his head briefly. For good measure he held out both hands palms facing the chief to show he meant no harm. The chief gave a curt grunt as though this was adequate but not amazing. Blyth wondered whether he was expected to cut out his own heart and hand it to the man in a silver bowl, but he suppressed his rising anger. He was surrounded by strangers in their own home, and he didn't need the inconvenience of a fight, even if he was sure his magic would prevail.

"You may rise," Gharath told him quietly.

Blyth stood up, retrieving his staff as he did so. He didn't trust this clan as far as he could throw a spear, which really wasn't very far.

The chief barked an order.

"You must hand over your staff while you are here," Gharath translated.

"I will do no such thing."

"Then you must leave."

The air practically crackled with tension as the chief and his blue-cloaked associate watched them, uncomprehending. Other men around the edge of the hut appeared ready for action.

"In the dark? In winter? If your chief wishes me dead, can he not order me cut down with swords and hasten the end?"

"He does not wish you dead, but he does not trust you either."

"I helped you catch a fine deer, which will feed everyone here and more besides.

"Yes, you did."

"Did you tell him this?" Blyth asked Gharath.

"We did, but everyone is a bit mistrustful because of the way you helped us catch it. You used magic, and that makes you dangerous."

"You're carrying a sword and shield, throwing spears, a bow, and a sling," Blyth observed. "Who do you say is dangerous?"

"Oh, come now. You can see my weapons, and you could see if I tried to use them. But magic is silent, swift, and unpredictable."

"You also have a knife strapped to each leg, inside your leg wraps."

"You noticed them?"

"I notice a lot. I notice you are not afraid to use magic yourselves," Blyth glanced at 'blue-cloak'.

"We have our magos and he is powerful believe me, but he is ours and he seeks to protect us. We do not know if the same is true of you, and the Kin-Father does not want to take any chances. You leave the staff until you leave the village."

Blyth thought briefly. There was still much he could do without his staff, but little chance of survival out there in the cold winter night, even with it. He relented and handed the staff to Gharath, who handed it to the blue-cloaked magos.

8

The roundhouse where Blyth slept was huge, with an upper floor where the everyday business of cooking and eating went on, as well as where everyone slept. The animals were kept on the ground floor, where they could keep warm, out of the bitter wind, and in turn, their body heat warmed the people above. The occupants included Gharath and his family, several other families, and servants. Blyth slept fitfully and woke feeling tired and irritable. He decided to leave as soon as he could recover his staff. He felt with his mind for Blodwyth; he had a sense that she was away in the direction to the left of the rising sun, but he also felt a sense that she had passed this way. He was on the right path, that much seemed certain. He ate some bread, and a thin broth, with the other occupants of the house and he talked to Gharath to get more information.

"What lands lie in that direction?" he gestured broadly towards the east.

"From here to the sea are the lands of my people. The high-chief holds the high ground a day's journey from here, in winter, and then it is another day to the coast in almost any direction."

"And beyond the sea?"

"Merchants trade with the lands on the far side of the sea. I heard tell the lands there are even colder than here and are icebound for longer. They have tin though, and some other things which are not obtainable here. Mostly they take surplus grain and bonded servants. We get our fair share of captives from raids," he added with a suitable air of pride for the prowess of his tribe's warriors.

Blyth, however, was not in the mood to congratulate. "Do your raiders ever reach as far as Ynys-Mona?" he asked, with a trace of bitterness in his tone.

"Not ours, that would be raiders from the lands of the Novantae, they trade through here sometimes. In fact, not half a moon since, they came through."

"Did they have a young woman with them, copper hair, about this tall, green eyes?"

"I wasn't here when they passed, but there are usually small groups, mostly women and children. The men prefer to fight to the death, so I am told," he laughed.

Blyth seethed internally, but uncharacteristically, he remained outwardly calm. "When can I get my staff back and be on my way?" he asked.

"I think, as soon as you wish," Gharath replied.

Blyth was escorted to the gates of the village before being handed his staff by a servant of the chief. The blue cloaked mage looked on disdainfully. Blyth wondered how much power the mage really had. He knew many tricks to fool ordinary warriors, and farmers into thinking you possessed magic. He also knew the difference between that and real magic. Blyth was still burning with outrage at whoever it was who had taken his Blodwyth from their peaceful island, and as far as he was concerned, this village had watched her pass through and done nothing.

The fact that trading in slaves, or 'bonded servants', was a way of life among every tribe that Blyth had ever known, and indeed, there were slaves doing the menial chores at Ynys-Mona so the Deru-Weidi could concentrate on more spiritual activities, was neither here nor there to him at this moment. He turned and walked a few paces away from the village and then, without warning, he turned and uttered a roar. With a sweep of his staff he directed all his pent-up rage at the assembly. A fierce wind whirled up from nowhere, in a focussed storm that knocked the chief and the mage, and the rest of the warriors, off their feet, covering them all in a huge amount of snow and ice.

Blyth said nothing, but turned and walked away, still burning with rage. Nobody attempted to chase after him. He was slightly disappointed at that.

9

Kaito rode up to the Deru-Weidi camp on Ynys-Mona, accompanied by Teague, Abbon, and Elarch, as well as their new companion, Aesos, the young man who had been with the band of robbers who had attacked them. He had begged to go with Kaito, who had agreed, after reaching into the lad's mind and finding him to be sincere. He was too old to train to become a Deru-Weido, but Kaito saw potential for him nevertheless.

There was a flurry of activity as word spread that Kaito himself had come to the camp. Eventually, he was met by Llwyd, Alisa, Telamonos, and Dwbrana, as well as other teachers and students, gathering to greet an old friend, or to meet for the first time the oldest and wisest living man they had ever heard tell of.

"You should have let us know you were coming, Kaito," Llwyd protested, as the horses were led away to be fed and groomed.

"I don't like to make a fuss. I am merely returning these two acolytes, and bringing this young lady, and, additionally this young man, here."

Elarch stepped forward confidently, Aesos less so. They were led away, while Kaito was taken to the large central house and pressed to drink, and eat, while he discussed his hopes for Elarch, which were straightforward, and Aesos, which were more difficult because he did not really know himself what he hoped for.

Llwyd and the others were not to be denied a chance to discuss in infinite detail everything that Kaito knew, or rather, was prepared to tell them, and to impart every scrap of news they could to him. The updates on Blyth took the longest, and were, at times, the most painful for Kaito to hear. Bellenos had long since departed across the western sea and the fire crackled brightly as the conversation continued, unabated, into the night. Kaito seemed bright and alert even as the others began to flag. Eventually, Llwyd showed him to a sleeping area that had been set aside for him. It was more comfortable than his sleeping quarters in his own house, having an abundance of soft and supple furs of the best quality. He slept well and awoke before Bellenos had reached the horizon - before his hosts in fact - and he had brewed a morning infusion before everyone was fully awake.

He passed cups around, and then said, "I must leave this morning, I still have a long journey ahead. Quite probably longer than I can imagine, and the longer I wait to leave, the longer it will get."

"You are going in search of Blyth then?" Alisa asked, with considerable foresight.

"I am."

Telamonos looked grave, "Do you think he is still alive?"

"I know he is. I can sense him." Kaito smiled wryly, "I can even sense anger, and destruction."

"Oh yes, that's Blyth alright," interjected Llwyd.

"He is too much like his father," Kaito looked down. "Too much like me," he glanced at Llwyd.

"If only he were like you, Kaito. He has such power. More power even than Trethiwr, I think, but also he is more emotional than Trethiwr, quicker to anger certainly, and that is something to behold."

Kaito looked levelly at Llwyd and spoke softly.

"You are young, Llwyd. You did not know me when I was a young man. My clan could not control me, I was exactly as Blyth is now. Powerful with magic that nobody else understood, there were mages then, as now, but none with anything like the powers I possessed. I killed a warrior in my clan who angered me. He took a piece of meat which I felt was mine, and I just stared at him. As I stared, he choked, and died. Nobody sought to blame me, but I knew.

"I left one day, when I was calm enough to know it was the best thing for them, and for me. I travelled across the known world, through the lands of the Romani, Helleni, Parthi, and beyond, reaching tribes as yet still barely known, even to the Romani. I travelled as far as it is possible to travel in the direction where Bellenos arises in the morning. The people there had tales of mysterious lands beyond the Eastern ocean, but none had travelled that way and returned to tell of them.

"There, I studied with a great wise man who taught me how to control my power, and only to use it for good. His name is hard to say in our language; Dzunsho is close. He quoted a long-dead mage, named Tzi. He talked of the philosophy of one who he called Gautama and said that it favoured calm meditation to reach a state where one can be with Lugh, the shining one, even in life. I sought out teachers of this philosophy and spent another year learning to control my own mind and emotions above all else.

"When I returned to my own village, I was not instantly welcomed, but I was patient, and eventually was fully accepted by almost everyone. The person you see before you now is what Blyth may one day become, if I can help him find the right path; the path to the shining one, in life, and not in death, as his father chose."

Kaito finished his drink, placed the cup down, and stood up to leave, "I need to speak with Teague and Abbon before I go," he said.

The young men were summoned and Kaito waved the elders away.

10

"I understand that you both learned to transform into animals from a far distant land?"

"I can transform into something the Romani call tigris," Teague admitted, "but it causes me to feel bad. I can't exactly explain it."

"I learned to change into a creature which is like a small but powerful man, all covered in hair, with hands for feet. I never found out what the Romani call it."

"Simius, I think," Kaito said. "Show me the transformation, please."

"I too find it uncomfortable to change into him. I feel sick for a long time afterwards. I've never talked about it, but since Teague has said the same…" he trailed off.

"You found the animals already caged, did you not?" Kaito probed.

"Yes," Teague admitted, knowing where this line of questioning was going.

"And Gwenn taught you to learn everything there was to know about the animal before making the kill and conducting the rituals?"

"She did," they both muttered, heads hung low as Abbon also realised the point Kaito was about to make.

"Therefore, you know now why these transformations cause you discomfort."

They nodded.

"And you also know that the only way to make them work properly for you is to go and seek out these animals in their natural environment and observe them closely until you know everything you can about them."

They both began to look up, but not yet fully certain how to proceed. A quizzical look passed over their faces and Kaito continued.

"Teague, your journey is relatively easy, in as much as the lands you must visit are well known and highly civilised. You will be able to converse in Hellenic for almost the entire journey albeit with many shifts of dialect. You must journey east from the lands of the Romani, through their province of Asia, and beyond to the land called Parthia. Sometimes powerful men hunt the tigris to prove their strength and courage. But you need to observe it, not hunt. It lives in forests, mostly to the east of Parthia and beyond. They are not easy to see, never mind observe at length. That will be your most difficult challenge."

He looked next at Abbon.

"Your journey is less clear, since I do not know enough to give you more than the most basic guidelines. If you could show me the creature briefly it would perhaps help."

Abbon concentrated and transformed into the chimpanzee, although it looked sickly and when he transformed back he felt weak.

"It wasn't like this at the start," Abbon explained as Teague intimated his agreement.

"I have no experience of this, but it doesn't matter. You should both avoid attempting this transformation until you have done the necessary study."

Both young men indicated their enthusiastic agreement with this. Kaito addressed Abbon specifically again.

"Begin by travelling to the far side of the southern sea, to the red-lands where your father last travelled. The Helleni call it Aegyptus. Begin in the city of Alexandria and start asking. There are simians there, but none quite like that one. Hellenic is widely spoken in Aegyptus, but you may have to journey beyond their lands, perhaps beyond the land they call Kush. I cannot say much about these places, but your father journeyed there and returned, so I presume you will have as good a chance as any of coming back safely. What I have less hope of, is that you will find your 'hairy little man' easily."

"When should we begin this journey?" Teague asked.

"Now?" Kaito paused, "or never? You are men now; you must make your own decisions. Leave when you decide you want to. You will learn much on your journey, particularly if you remember that you have two eyes, and two ears, but only one mouth, and you should make use of them in those proportions."

Kaito smiled and swept out to find the elders and say his farewells.

"Go safely, Kaito. May Lugh and all the Gods watch over you," Llwyd said, by way of parting.

"They do my friend, they always do. Take good care of my horse while I am gone, please," he added.

11

Kaito engaged a good-sized fishing vessel to sail him north from the isle of Mona, as far as the isle of Manaw to the north. During the voyage, he sensed an awful rage in the mind of his quarry. The blood-kin magic, combined with Kaito's exceptional mental powers, gave him a uniquely detailed picture of events beyond his immediate horizon. There was no question of knowing exactly what was going on, in the way that being there would provide, but somewhere to the east, there had been an incident that enraged Blyth. Kaito had no way of knowing if Blyth was in danger but, if he were not, then whoever or whatever had annoyed him most certainly was. He needed to speed up his journey and catch up with Blyth soon.

There was only one way to travel at the speed he needed, so Kaito made his way towards the higher ground and away from the village and farms as far as possible. High in the hills, he found a stunted tree, denuded of leaves, contorted by the wind that blew up through the narrowing valley. It was as good a place to wait as any other. Kaito reached out with the tendrils of his mind, this time searching not for the presence of Blyth, but for a powerful and sophisticated mind, beyond the understanding of ordinary men. It would take some time, so Kaito leaned his staff against the stunted tree and draped his cloak over it, placing stones around the bottom edge to hold it down. It would have been a completely inadequate shelter without the addition of a little magic to make the cloak water and wind resistant. The few sticks he had collected on his way up the hill made a small fire and he was able to produce a passable brew. He nevertheless missed the comfort and familiarity of his house in the woods, further south, where winter's grip was neither as complete, nor lasted as long. He was heading further north, into lands that he barely knew, at the worst time of year. Kaito shivered and told himself he was too old to be doing this sort of thing anymore.

Bellenos had barely crested the horizon all day; although it had not set, it was out of sight, beyond the crest of the hill. The wind picked up, and it started to rain. The small fire smoked and spat. Kaito sighed and ventured out to find some more fuel before it was all soaked. Further up the slope was a ragged looking evergreen, with a badly damaged branch, which quickly gave up the fight against Kaito's tugging. He dragged it back, pleased to have enough fuel to keep going well into the night. As the sun began to set, he fed the fire and huddled closer to it, as the rain began to fall much harder.

Eventually, after what seemed like an age, he heard the deep thunderous crack of leathery wings beating against the air, lifting a huge creature like a cross between a giant lizard and an impossibly large bat. The dark red leathery wings looked black as they glistened and dripped in the moonlight.

'You requested my help, human?' The creature's thoughts entered Kaito's head as words that he could understand. He replied, in normal speech, though how the dragon interpreted those words was still a mystery to Kaito. He presumed the thoughts required to form the words were read directly by the dragon's huge, unfathomable mind.

"I thank you for coming to my aid. I must travel a long distance in a short time, and I beseech you to carry me there. I have nothing I can give you that you might desire but, as always, I pledge willingly to protect your kind should the opportunity arise, and to encourage those who follow me to do the same. It is not much, given that you may live many times longer than I, and I shall always be in your debt."

'Well spoken human, but you know as well as I, that I might not be here at all, were it not for your compassion. I think it is I who is in your debt. Climb on.'

Kaito straddled the slender neck and the dragon lifted into the air with a few beats of its massive wings.

Kaito focussed his mind on Blyth. His thoughts were picked up by the dragon, guiding it without the need for clumsy directions. They swooped over the landscape in the darkness, almost silent but for the occasional crack of the great wings, which must have sounded like thunder to anyone standing below, in the pouring rain. Kaito stayed dry, thanks to magic, but not warm. There was no magical way to keep warm while flying through the winter night air on the back of a dragon, but there was no choice, and this way, a journey of a week could be reduced to a few hours, and the sun would be rising shortly after they landed.

'You are a rare human indeed. You care for those who are weak or helpless yet, with all your gifts, you do not seek power over others.'

"Power over others carries great responsibility. I believe the path to the light of Lugh requires doing good, and thinking pure thoughts, in every aspect of life. Leadership requires that one must make difficult, almost impossible, decisions. The more men one rules over, the more and harder those decisions become. I have learned the only way to maintain the inner peace and calm I need is to keep myself apart from others, and only influence gently, from afar. If I could do what I have to do now without leaving my home I would have done so."

12

Kaito approached the village from the west, with the sun rising behind the palisade, lighting up the heavy frost and snowdrifts like a vast hoard of jewels. He was still very cold, and really needed to sit by a fire and drink a hot brew. As he drew closer it was clear that the guards at the gate were on full alert, bristling with glinting spears. 'The foolish man strikes where the fly has already been and closes the pen when the sheep are in the fields.' Kaito thought to himself.

He approached, smiling, with palms facing forward, his staff slung on his back. If these warriors had recently been attacked by a mage, by Blyth in fact, then they would mistrust him by association. So, the best defence is no defence at all. Well, no visible defence at least.

Once he was within shouting distance, one of the gatekeepers called to Kaito to stop. The words were somewhat alien, but Kaito understood the meaning clearly enough.

'A smile can save many problems, and silence may help avoid them,' he thought, as he approached further, with a serene and sincere smile on his face.

When he was within spear range, the gatekeepers hefted their spears, preparing to throw. Kaito emphasised his forward-facing palms and smiled as he continued to approach. The gatekeepers looked at each other, bewildered. Nobody ever did this. When you told them to stop, and threatened them with spears, people stopped and maybe even went away, or they attacked. Nobody had ever walked calmly towards them like this, unarmed, and without at least a shield.

They looked at each other, and both agreed without a word, to summon the kin-father and the agos. They turned to call out and already other villagers were coming, having heard the earlier shouts. Among them were the two most senior men, who would take charge, much to the gatekeepers' relief.

"It is another magos, Kin-father, like the one who just left."

"He is older. Do you suppose him wiser?"

"Perhaps, or more powerful? We must stop him before he finishes what the youth began."

The kin-father understood, and he gave an order to the warriors. Thirty spears were hefted and launched almost at once. Kaito stopped and waited, motionless, his palms still facing the warriors in the universal gesture of peace. Many spears fell short, or wide, some were on target, yet none quite hit their mark. There were faint gasps, and puzzled expressions from the warriors. The kin-father gave the order again, and thirty more spears were launched; this time, many more were on target. Kaito stood unmoved and unhurt, even as the last spear fell kicking up a spray of glittering frosty snow.

In the silence that followed, Kaito walked forward once more, still smiling, still showing his palms, until he was almost at the gates. Some warriors began to prepare rocks to throw down upon his head but, at this point, the kin-father felt the urge to meet this man who was apparently impervious to spears.

"Open the gates! Allow him inside!"

Kaito was immensely glad of this, as he was exhausted from using many powerful defensive spells at once. The wooden gates were drawn open to admit the small wiry old mage in the rich blue cloak. Still smiling, not the triumphal smile of a victor, but the sincere smile of one who can love even his enemies, Kaito walked into the village. He headed towards the obvious centre of power: the magos, with his magnificent blue cloak shot through with silver and gold thread, and the kin-father, in polished leather and gleaming armour, bristling with fine weapons and laden with silver torcs.

And now the language barrier loomed. Since Kaito had only briefly passed through these lands before, he knew only the barest essentials. He placed his palms together and bowed, then opened his palms to the front again and spoke a faltering phrase he had been taught a long time ago.

Men of the Wise Oak

"Greetings, great chief. I know not the good words. I am of a wrong tribe. I can talk like the Brigantii."

The kin-father smiled at this feeble attempt at speaking his language but accepted the effort had been made. Gharath was called. He had been punished for bringing Blyth into their village, but he was one of the few who spoke the barbaric language of the Brigantii far to the south west.

The magos spoke to Gharath, who stepped forward and said, "One who looked like you, but younger, passed through here, and did us great harm. Why should we trust you any more than he?"

"You may tell your mage, that I seek to stop the youth from doing further harm. Please tell him, he may take my staff while I am here, and all I seek is shelter, a warm fire, and some food. I can pay in gold." He held out a gold arm-torc to show he meant it.

The kin-father's eyes lit up at the sight of so much gold, and the magos knew well enough not to deny him his prize. It would raise the status of the whole tribe, as long as this old man was true to his word.

A servant took the staff admiring, as he did so, the translucent stone embedded into the top; seemingly studded with frozen ferns which seemed to grow and glow inside the stone.and Kaito was brought to the kin-father's house, where he finally got warm beside a roaring fire, and drank an infusion of his own, which he shared freely with the kin-father, the magos, and Gharath, who had to be there as interpreter. He even left them a small supply.

"Tell me, exactly what happened?" he asked.

The magos told the story of Blyth's visit, and Kaito looked suitably shocked at his behaviour. He asked which way Blyth had headed, although he already had a very clear sense of his direction. If Kaito concentrated, he could sense a rippling effect, as of sunlight on water. 'So, Blyth was heading for the coast. For what reason? To take ship? Or had he run Blodwyth to ground there?'

"… and another day's journey to the coast," Gharath finished.

Kaito was drawn out of his reverie and back to the here-and-now. He desperately needed to rest and eat. He also needed to learn a few more useful phrases and words in the language of this tribe, in case there was no one to interpret at the next village. It was already getting dark and a fierce wind had blown up. If Blyth was seeking to take ship, then he would not sail tonight. If he did manage to leave in the morning there were still ways to catch him up but, even with all his power, Kaito was not fool enough to try to walk across open moors in a blizzard, at night. The fire crackled invitingly and his hosts, who had warmed to the older man, with the twinkling eyes and the calm demeanour, talked long into the night, telling old stories in their own language, while Gharath translated as best he could for Kaito.

13

Blyth boarded the trading vessel in a hurry. The plank was taken away, the last of the cargo of grain was being stowed in the hold, and the captain shouted orders to the crew as the ship slipped out with the ebbing tide. Oarsmen pulled and sweated, while the sails were still being unfurled to catch the breeze. It looked set fair for a swift crossing.

He thought back over the incidents of the previous day. The trader he met had recently sold a group of slaves at the harbour. Blyth knew this, because he had reached into the man's mind. He had seen Blodwyth's face, terrified; seen her tied to others just like her. When he left, the trader was still alive, but he might have been better off dead, without enough of his mind left to remember his own name.

Kaito, meanwhile, hastened his steps as he felt the power that had surged from Blyth into the unknown man's mind.

The boat was hugging the coast. Blyth looked out across the cold grey sea, in the direction where the sun rose in summer, towards where he knew Blodwyth was:

captive, mistreated, scared. He cornered the ship's captain.

"Why are we heading along the coast? We should be going that way." He pointed to the distant horizon.

The captain rubbed his beard with a calloused hand and looked hard into Blyth's eyes.

"Have you ever been to sea, boy?"

Blyth looked away towards where he felt Blodwyth's presence.

The captain went on, "We sail along the coast because if we sail off across the open sea we lose sight of land before sunset, and we are at the mercy of the Gods for at least two nights. Unless you can command the waves, and call upon Manannan for aid?"

"I cannot," Blyth said quietly, still staring at the ocean and not returning the captain's steely gaze. The oars were shipped as the wind filled the sails. They would only be used if the wind dropped or was blowing in the wrong direction.

"I told you the crossing would take seven nights and, barring disaster, I will keep true to my word. I've made this voyage every moon through a dozen summers. Warriors make the crossing in their long boats for raiding sorties. For them it is a rite of passage, to prove they are worthy. Some come home with stolen silver or, if they are very successful, captured women. Others never return, they lie at the bottom of the sea, and their souls feast with Manannan and not Lugh. Me? I prefer to trade and, unlike those warriors, I have to make the journey again.

In fact, they just make my task harder because wherever they strike, the people have less trust, and more anger."

Blyth sighed but said nothing. He just continued staring out at the horizon, willing the space between him and Blodwyth to close up.

"The journey will pass faster if you do something useful with your time."

Blyth stared silently at the sea as it hissed and slapped at the tightly sewn planks. The captain left him with his thoughts. He had paid his passage in gold; if he wanted to do nothing for the whole voyage that was his choice.

Blyth did indeed keep himself to himself for the entire seven days of the voyage. He stayed below decks for the most part and ate barely any food that was brought to him. When he stepped ashore, he looked ashen and gaunt, like a dead man walking. He was naturally slender, but now his bones showed through skin as thin as sausage-casing. The staff he carried looked almost larger than he did. The crew feared for him but for themselves even more. It was as though they had transported a soul to the land of the dead and they shuddered, glad to see the back of him, and hoped never to see him again.

14

When Gwenn had parted company with Caesar, and gone in search of her friend Titus, she had no idea how difficult the task would prove. Asking around bore little fruit. She realised that she had never learned more than Titus' praenomen, and without his Gens, or cognomen, she could not distinguish him from thousands of others in every town. She did what she had done before, when she had arrived in Rome; she set up a small shop in a low rent area of the city of Capua, offering her knowledge and skills to the sick. As always, she found that her first customers were often too poor to pay her, but as word spread of her unique abilities, she reached more and more, usually women, who could. It kept her financially secure, and she got to hear all the local gossip.

Epona therefore had little difficulty finding her old friend, when she began asking around in the forum of Capua, and she was more than gratified to find that the smaller town had a fresher smell than the great city of Rome itself. As she had done previously, she breezed into the little apothecary shop, unannounced, towards the end of the day, and smiled as Gwenn recognised her, with obvious pleasure.

"The Gods have blessed me," she said. "I've missed you, despite all your grumbling. Have you come to drag me away again, or have you decided the Romani have their merits after all?"

"Gwenn, leuka! I can't say I have any more love for the Romani than before, although I confess they may not all be completely evil, but I swear, if you don't have some of their best wine to hand, I won't be responsible for my actions. I have come all the way from the house of Kaito at his behest, months of travelling, to keep you safe from yourself, if I can. I can no longer fathom his motivations. He is either wiser than we all suspect, or a crazy fool."

"Kaito is no fool," Gwenn admitted, pouring the asked for wine. "Do you think he has gone mad?"

"No. Perhaps not, but he thinks you have."

"What?" Gwenn slammed her cup on the table.

"Well, that's maybe an exaggeration, but he is worried about you."

"Tell the great wise-oak that I can take care of myself, thank you very much."

"Tell him yourself! I've been back and forth across the world, running errands for him, quite enough already."

"I'm happy enough here. I came to see Titus for no other reason than to catch up with an old friend, but I like it here. The people are friendly, not like the Romani in Roma; a lot of them don't even like the Romani. Old rivalries. Centuries ago, this town was more powerful than

Roma. They were a different tribe, just as tribes are separate in Gaul or Pretan. To them, it's as if they were the Dwr-y-tryges and they have been ruled by the Eceni for generations," Gwenn said, well aware that Epona was born into the Eceni, and married into the Dwr-y-tryges.

"Well the wine is passable and the air is sweeter than in Rome. There are worse places to make your home. However, Kaito believes you have fallen under the spell of Gaius Julius Caesar. He thinks that you tried to force his mind and, untrained as he is, his mind resisted, and broke you," Epona said.

Gwenn was silent, but evidently considering her reaction. She ran through events in her mind; deep down, she knew the truth of it, but she hated to think that she was a victim, and not a willing client, of the charismatic young patrician. But that was it, that was the point, he had kharisma, that magical ability to sway people to his will. Hadn't he done so countless times, when she had accompanied him to Asia? And how else could anyone have treated the Cilician pirates with such disdain and hauteur? He had actually ordered them to praise his poetry, shouted at them to be silent when he wanted to sleep. He had got his ships in Bithynia as well, although she felt certain her own contribution had been significant.

And then, like the final ward of a lock clicking into place, she realised, as if it was for the first time, that she had become his slave. She, Gwenn of the Helvetii, daughter of Durnako of the Cimbri, had willingly become a slave, and been proud to be his slave. But then, she reasoned, he was a Roman patrician, and she had only chosen to become his slave so that she could fulfil her mission to keep watch over him. Yes; she had done everything willingly and under her own control. The Romani were a civilised people, incredible engineers, writers, thinkers, planners, and warriors; but of magic they had none. Oh, a wealth of Gods and rituals. Augurs and priests a-plenty, but not the powerful magic of the Deru-Weidi mages. How then could some boy overcome her mind? It was madness to suggest it.

At last, Gwenn replied to Epona. "I am quite sure Kaito is mistaken on this occasion." She smiled and finished her wine. "Come on, let's close up and I will show you where I am staying. It's not much, but it is clean, and doesn't stink like a latrine."

15

Kaito arrived at the port several days after Blyth had sailed. He had learned enough of the language to find somewhere to stay and someone with whom he could communicate. As was so often the case, there were many words in common although even these were pronounced differently with different inflections. Learn the inflections, and the language began to fall into place surprisingly quickly. It was certainly easier to learn than some. He had travelled along the great silk road, beyond Parthia to the land at the eastern edge of the world. He had traded with a people who called themselves the Han, and their language was quite unlike any he had encountered. Even the Helleni had some very strange ways with words, although once you had mastered their language you could travel almost anywhere and still be understood.

His first task, as he saw it, was to try to undo the damage done by his great-grandson. The merchant was not too hard to find. He was sitting outside a hut looking emaciated and filthy, a vacant expression on his face, flies hovering round his eyes unheeded. Kaito tried speaking to him but got no response. Gently he felt inside the man's mind. If it could be explained in terms we might understand, it was a mess like a tangled ball of wool. But he could see small ways to lessen the damage. He worked away for some time until the effort exhausted him. It took three days before he felt the man was properly able to take care of himself again. He had lost precious time, but the need to heal was ingrained and, in old age, Kaito felt as though he had to build up a store of good deeds more than ever before.

Preparing to sail east in the wake of Blyth, Kaito sought out the largest boat he could. He was in luck; twenty oars, and a huge hide sail snapping in a frisky westerly. Grain sacks were being loaded by a gang of workers. Kaito approached and hailed the captain in the local dialect. He called back, but in another language: Cimbric! Kaito switched with ease to the language of Gwenn's father, a language he was as comfortable with as Latin or Greek.

"Sail you homeward? To Cimbria?"

"Aye!"

When a suitable gap opened between the dock workers Kaito stepped onto the loading plank, nimbly for one so old, and came on board. In a softer voice he asked the captain, "How much to sail as the whale swims?"

The captain looked at him through fierce blue eyes under bushy blonde brows drawn together.

"I have gold." Kaito hefted a bag tied to his belt.

"Does your gold float?"

"It does not."

"Can your gold feed seven hungry children when their father lies at the bottom of the sea?"

"It cannot."

"Then my fine mage, if that you be, unless you can command the waves and call the Gods to our aid, we must sail by the coast as we always do and make the best time we can."

"But the wind is from the west, and a strong wind it is. We could be in your home port by the sunset after next. Imagine the smiles on your children's faces when their pater comes home days before time, and with a purse full of gold."

"It's a fair wind, I'll mark that. But should this fine wind drop? Then what?"

"It won't."

"You command the winds do you?"

Kaito had rested well. He had saved up all his energy. He raised a hand, and the breeze dropped to nothing. He knew that he would pay dearly for this later, but he would be able to rest and recover. The reaction of the captain was reward enough. His eyebrows drew closer together, and his blue eyes burned. Kaito lowered his hand and the breeze rose again filling the sail with a crack.

"Who *are* you?" the captain asked awestruck.

"When do we sail?" Kaito asked, holding out the bag of gold.

"The tide is turning now. The last of the sacks are coming on." He took the bag and called out his orders in a booming voice, as the last of the dock workers scurried to shore.

"Cast off!! Sail square! Oarsmen to rest for now!"

The crewmen went about their work, and the ship began ever so slowly to ease away from the dock and out to sea. The captain turned to a man who was, presumably, his second in command.

"Double rations for the crew; we sail as the whale swims and reach home by the sunset after next."

"But captain…"

"Pray to the Gods; they seem disposed to listen to this mage."

"Yes, captain."

The crossing went smoothly, and Kaito swapped stories with the captain and his mate as they sipped his special infusions. The crew were ambivalent: worried at making the crossing direct, but also pleased to be getting double rations, and excited at the thought of making the voyage in half the time. Even the oarsmen, all bonded servants with no choice in anything, were pleased as the strong westerly kept up all day and well into the next after sunset. They were required to row for a few hours before the wind picked up again. By late in the second day, the lookout sighted land and the relief swept through the ship in an almost palpable wave. The sail was adjusted to change course slightly. The oarsmen, as keen as anyone else to reach land, could not be dissuaded from rowing, and the captain had little desire to stop them. It was long before sunset when they pulled alongside the dock and Kaito stepped ashore as nimbly as a mountain goat on a hill-path. The crew wished him well and prayed to their Gods that they would have the pleasure of his presence on their ship again.

16

Blyth was a shadow: good for nothing. In his mind there was a buzzing, white noise of hopelessness. He felt worthless. There was no point in eating, no point in worrying about pain or discomfort, because he was not worth caring about. He wandered aimlessly, blindly, along a street which he vaguely imagined was the main path through his childhood village of Ba-dun.

He saw someone he knew from his childhood. It was Cuilleana. She was the mother of a young warrior, Rodokoun, who had been a rival to Blyth for Blodwyth. She was also the mother of Ruthgem, a flame-haired girl who had been taken prisoner when a meeting of chiefs had gone wrong. Then she had helped Blyth and his brothers escape from Ba-dun when the mage had their father killed. Strong feelings surged through Blyth as they had not done for many days. He had felt nothing: not anger, nor sadness, not joy or hope; just emptiness. An abyss, like the great swirling void of the first times, the time before time. Blyth's Deru-Weidi training took over and, in his mind, he recited the story in his head.

'From the void came Rekwos and time began. Darkness was created first, and the darkness prevailed for an unknowable amount of time because there was no passing of days and nights, no sun or moon, by which to measure. Then came Eiolewka, the first light, and from the union of Eiolewka with Rekwos came Dis Fater, the sky father who created the sky with his breath, and Deoghmachter, who lay down and became the Earth. But the earth was barren. So Dis Fater and Deoghmachter lay together and their coupling brought forth the first Gods. The waters of the birth filled the seas, and the rivers, and the lakes.'

But why was Cuilleana here, and why was she helping him? It didn't matter. He passed into unconsciousness.

———

When he woke, it was dark with just a small fire illuminating stone walls and flickering on the flame red hair of the woman who, of course, was not Cuilleana. He managed to lift his head and, whoever she was, she held a cup to his lips and a hot liquid moistened his cracked lips. Chamomile. It reminded him of home again. His mother, Epona, would make him drink all sorts of infusions of herbs when he was ill.

He lay back on the thick furs. 'Why bother', he thought, 'I'm not worth saving.' Then a vision flashed across his mind of Blodwyth. He remembered why he was here, why he had taken a fishing vessel to the island of Manaw, and sailed again to the lands of the Brigantii and beyond, why he had walked for months across a frozen landscape, meeting tribes he never knew existed, sailed again along rugged coasts on iron dark seas, and come to this place.

His thoughts were interrupted by the woman saying something in a strange language. Despite not recognising the words, he understood that she wanted him to drink and, in his weakened state, he couldn't resist the urgings of the woman who was like Cuilleana, someone who had helped him before, even though this wasn't her. His thoughts spun. He sipped the chamomile infusion and felt its warmth flow through him, physically and mentally soothing. He looked properly at his saviour; her eyes were green like Blodwyth's and she smiled at him.

The scent of something savoury wafted past his nostrils and he realised for the first time in many days that eating was something that could be enjoyable, something people did, that you had to do if you were to stay alive. As if she read his mind, not-Cuilleana filled a bowl with a hot pale-brown liquid. It was thick with the consistency of porridge. Blyth allowed her to spoon some into his mouth before taking the spoon from her. He could feed himself: he was a man not a baby. It tasted like the best food he had ever tasted, although it was just barley, oats, peas, and leftover meat and fat from previous meals.

She spoke again, this time in a different language. It sparked off memories in Blyth's brain until the right connections fired. 'Hellenic; she's speaking Hellenic.'

"Yes, yes, I speak Hellenic," he replied to her question.

"My name is Rauthrid of the Cimbri, daughter of Ulfr of the Cimbri and Commia of the Attrebates."

Blyth took in the serene face, the rich clothing, the use of herbs and good food. He looked around in the half light and, yes, there was his staff leaning against the wall, and next to it, another, shorter, topped with a different stone, but clearly the staff of a mage.

"You're a healer?"

"Of course, and you too I presume?"

"Yes."

"We normally take better care of ourselves than you have been."

"I... couldn't think of... it's hard to explain. I felt that nothing mattered, least of all me."

Rauthrid kept her face impassive and said nothing.

Blyth went on, "I've felt bad before, felt useless when I've made a foolish mistake, but nothing quite this bad. It felt like... *I felt like* the swirling void before time began. Like Khaos."

Rauthrid looked concerned.

"I have heard of that feeling before. It is rare; more common among those of us with the gift. There was a young mage many years ago when I was scarcely more than a child. He looked a bit like you in fact. He was very powerful, but the Gods had cursed and blessed him in equal measure. I only met him twice, at great gatherings. On the first occasion he was in a dark place and was obviously suffering just as you were when I found you, the next time he was vibrant and excited and talking about his travels in far off lands. I wonder what happened to him? I talk too much, sorry. So, what's your name then, and what brings you to the land of ice and water?"

"Ice and water?"

"The story goes this land used to be green and fertile, but then the floods came. Almost everyone left when their farms were drowned, and their houses filled with water. I understand that those who left never found lands to settle in. They were eventually all killed by the Romani." She spat venomously. "A few stayed, but the ice makes it hard to grow crops, and although some of the waters receded, we still have less land than my father's parents had to farm or hunt in. Look at me, I'm talking again, and I still don't know your name!"

"Blyth. Blyth of the Dwr-y-tryges, son of Trethiwr of the Dwr-y-tryges and Epona of the Eceni."

"Trethiwr! That was his name. Oh, so that explains a lot. How is your father?"

"He died."

"I'm sorry."

Rauthrid looked genuinely sorry, but there was an awkward silence as neither could think of anything useful to say. Then there was a call from outside and Rauthrid said she had to go but would be back soon. It was not clear whether she or Blyth was the more grateful for the interruption as she picked up her staff and hurried out.

17

Blyth's recovery was as rapid and complete as his descent into the void, to khaos as he himself called it, had been. He was jovial, talkative, irrepressible; exchanging stories and jokes in Hellenic, and learning key words and phrases in Cimbric, recognising in them some of the things that Gwenn said from time to time. He found himself growing fond of Rauthrid, and it was clear the feeling was mutual, although Blyth still kept his strongest feelings for Blodwyth. On the third day he felt out for her and sensed she was near, but still to the East. He prepared to leave and, after a long and lingering goodbye to Rauthrid, he resumed his quest.

The going was tough; ice and snow gave way only to open water. Many small lakes and ponds, which he could go around, and then open sea which he could not. There were fishing boats which were willing to take him across for small payments, or favours. Imbolc had passed, Blyth wasn't even sure when, but he could tell the sun was setting later, and rising earlier every day, yet there was still ice and snow as far as the eye could see. The land was still quite flat here but, in the distance, he could see hills rising to hazy blue mountains. He headed north and east. In the distance rising smoke led, after a few hours, to a cluster of low dark buildings on a raised platform over a crystal blue lake. The largest building was circular with stone walls and roofed over with timber and turf. It housed cattle and pigs sheltering from the icy grip of a winter that seemed unwilling to give way to spring. The sun was shining though. Rivers and streams were overflowing with meltwater, freezing cold and laden with dark silt from distant mountains.

Blyth hailed the village from a distance. He was in a good frame of mind, feeling neither rage nor sadness. Nor did he feel the dark void. He felt the sun on his face, and the warmth reflected his own emotional state. He even laughed, for no discernible reason. Blodwyth was close by. She was here, he was sure of it. There were no walls, little evidence of any fortifications. It was just a small village: a dozen huts, a large central longhouse, and the cattle byre. At home in the land of the Dwr-y-Tryges, there was no need to bring animals indoors except in the worst of winter nights. Here it seemed to be the norm. The overpowering acrid smell of animal excrement assailed his nostrils.

"Hello!" he called again in the language of the Cimbri.

A woman emerged from a hut holding something, possibly wool. A farmer wandered down towards the village from somewhere to the right; he was carrying a farm tool, some sort of hand plough, Blyth thought. There was no threat, no danger, just people working the land, with nothing to fear. They probably had too little wealth for warriors to bother raiding them, so far from anywhere important and with winter losing its grip so late in the year. It would be Beltane soon, and there would still be ice on the lower slopes; still in the mountains after Lughnasadh, Blyth guessed correctly.

He walked towards the woman with his arms open, cloak thrown back to show he had no weapons. None save his staff that is. She showed curiosity rather than fear. As he drew closer he spoke again in Cimbric, "May the Gods smile upon you and your family. I am Blyth of the Dwr-y-tryges and I seek food and shelter on my journey."

The woman evidently understood him and replied, "Welcome Blyth of the Dwr-y-tryges, I am Biarnafa. Come." She led the way back to the house and ushered him inside.

A woman was stirring a big black pot over an open hearth, when she looked up her eyes widened, and she dropped the stirrer.

Blyth spoke first, "Blodwyth!"

He looked around, his face growing thunderous, but Blodwyth was quick to spot his rising temper.

"Blyth!" she spoke, urgently, in their own language. "Whatever you think of the people who took me from Mona, these are not those people. They have been more than kind to me. Their life is hard, and they have nothing but what you see around you," she winced visibly as she stood up.

"What's the matter, what did they do to you?" Blyth looked worried.

"They did nothing Blyth. They helped me. This is more your doing…" she stood aside, and Blyth noticed, for the first time, a baby sleeping next to where she had been seated.

18

Biarnafa bustled around preparing a hot drink and filling cups, as Blyth stared at the baby and then at Blodwyth. He was speaking his own language and it felt good to pronounce words in the old familiar way of his childhood, without fear of getting muddled or having to say things slowly and repeat things.

"Is it your baby?"

"It is mine *and* yours, Blyth."

"But how did…?" Blyth scarcely knew where to begin asking what happened. It took Blodwyth a long time to relate the whole story. Of how she had been out in the early morning, awaiting the return of Bellenos, when she had been snatched by the raiders. That she had been taken across the sea and, instead of the usual way of being sold to the first village where she would become a bonded servant, she was traded several times and continued travelling with other traders. Perhaps they recognised in her some skills they wanted, or perhaps the opposite; she did not have the skills that villages were seeking. Either way, she was taken further and further east. She had hidden her pregnancy, not sure what the traders would do if they found out; would they kill her, or the baby? Somehow, she had found herself in a marketplace and had been bought by a farmer, who had brought her here. The farmer, Biarni, and his wife Biarnafa had scarcely asked any physical work of her, even though there was much that needed doing. She had been well treated and Biarnafa was a good midwife.

Blyth looked at his child and, as almost every father has done for thousands of years before and since, he felt a flood of overpowering emotions that could not be put into words.

The man Blyth had seen carrying the farm tool entered and broke Blyth's reverie. He had blonde hair fading to silver, and thinning, but an impressive beard and moustaches braided with a few small amber beads. Deep lines creased his pale weatherworn skin, and piercing blue eyes gazed out from under bushy unkempt brows. Blodwyth spoke in Cimbric to tell Blyth this was Biarni, and the two men clasped wrists in greeting. Blodwyth continued explaining who Blyth was in full detail and Biarni, whose children must surely all be grown up now assuming he had them, congratulated Blyth on his son. It was at that point Blyth realised he had not even asked if it was a boy or a girl.

"Have you given him a name yet?" he asked Blodwyth.

"Not yet. I was waiting for you. I knew you were coming. I sort of felt it somehow."

"Aah, a woman's instinct," Biarni grunted, with a knowing wink for good measure, "There's no line sinks deep enough to measure a woman's mind."

Blyth hadn't heard the saying before, but it had a ring of truth, although he suspected there was more to it than that. Blodwyth had no magic like Blyth and his brothers. She was intelligent and educated; she knew the stories from the very beginning, from the time before time. She knew the healing herbs and useful plants, and she knew the Gods, even many of the small local Gods of rivers, and lakes, and strange rock shapes, and she knew the laws of the Gods, that ruled over the decisions made by leaders, even those who might be warring with their neighbours but would be bound by the same basic set of rules. But what Blodwyth could not do was go beyond what could be achieved just through learning. She had a staff, but that was for show, because a mage always has a staff, just as a chief always has magnificent gold torcs and the finest armour and cloak. But the power of her staff was only in the effect it had on those who respected the Deru-Weidi. She could not focus her energy through it to control the winds, or waves, or fire, or the ground beneath her feet. And yet, perhaps, she did have just a tiny vestige of magic. Perhaps she had felt his presence in the same way that he could feel her and find her across the span of many tribes and many seas, because they were blood kin.

19

Kaito was closer now than ever before. The direct crossing had brought him into the same harbour where Blyth had left his ship only days before. Kaito had felt the descent into the dark void that Blyth had endured, and also felt him recover. He cast an eye over the bustle of houses, grain stores, the marketplace, temple, and what he took to be the chief's house. Most of the important buildings were of stone and earth, with thick grass-topped roofs. Some were timber, and many of these were raised on stilts so the floor was above the ground. Kaito presumed that flooding was not uncommon here, or perhaps the flooding of the past had made local builders extra cautious. Today, at least, it was crisp and cold but dry and Bellenos, now setting over the sea behind him, marking the end of another day, had been making an effort to wipe the land clear of white and bring back the green.

Kaito stood out, in the way that foreigners in a strange land always do. A multitude of imperceptible differences in his clothing and equipment marked him out although, even in their own village, a mage does not automatically blend into the background.

He quickly located Rauthrid who, despite having no warning of his coming, was not particularly surprised once he had explained who he was. She remembered stories of Kaito, and knew he was the most powerful and wise of the Deru-Weidi. Without being asked she told him which way Blyth was headed, although Kaito knew as much anyway. She gave Kaito stew and he in turn produced an infusion which was somehow calming and stimulating in equal measure. She had not yet made the connection between Kaito and Blyth. When she did, she expressed her regret about Trethiwr. Kaito looked quiet and distant at talk of his late grandson, and Rauthrid resisted the urge to enquire as to the fate of Kaito's son, the father of Trethiwr. She reasoned that this man had presumably lived to see both his son and his grandson die, and now he was going all out to protect his great grandson. As much as death, particularly the death of children, was common and a fact of life that must be endured, she could not imagine how Kaito could avoid going to pieces, descending into the black void as Blyth had done, after such terrible losses. She kept her thoughts to herself as she sipped the hot liquid and felt it invigorate her.

"What's in this?" she asked.

"Chamomile, mint, chai, and traces of a rare plant from across the sea."

After a good night's sleep, Kaito was awake before dawn and had made an infusion before Rauthrid stirred. He left even as Bellenos began his journey across the heavens and as soon as he was clear of the village he transformed into a sleek grey wolf and pounded the ground in a series of great loping strides. When he came to a lake or river he switched fluidly to a creature known in his language as a water-dog although it was clearly not a dog - more like a pine marten - and completely at home in water. This way, Kaito covered the ground between him and Blyth faster than any other method, until he came to a wider stretch of sea that required a boat. Of all the transformations Kaito had mastered, none of them was a bird. He decided perhaps he should fix that, but then he wondered how many more winters he would live to see and whether it would be worth his while.

He found a settlement and soon managed to negotiate with a fisherman who was planning to set out to sea anyway. The crossing went smoothly and Kaito was grateful for a favourable wind. There was no way he had the strength to call up a wind now. He needed his energy for the transformations. Kaito was lost in his thoughts. Nothing worth having can be had for free, except the gifts of the Earth Mother, Sky Father, and the other Gods. Bellenos shone, the rains fell and the winds blew, the soil produced crops and the forest teemed with game, all for free. Sunsets, rainbows, waterfalls, and blossoming flowers were displays of the wonder of the Gods.

Then Kaito's thoughts turned to the Romani. They were surely the only people who would, if they could, charge for the privilege of watching the sun set. Only the Romani could claim to own land which they had never stepped upon. Their code of laws allowed a man to rule over people whom he had never met. For a year he would be called consul, a title which Kaito could only assume meant thief. The consul would be placed in charge of people whose language he refused to learn, and whose culture and religion he refused to acknowledge. His arrogance knew no bounds; he believed himself superior to every Celtic chief, to every Asian king, and even to the emperors of the land between two rivers. That arrogance, that unquestioned belief in the superiority of Roman blood, made them dangerous. They did not treat other peoples as human beings at all, but as inferior races, something *other*, something not fully human; and if you can believe that someone is less than human, then you no longer have to treat them as you would treat a human.

The Romani believed that no slave could give evidence without being tortured. Kaito had learned that torture never gets to the truth. He could see into the minds of others, with or without their permission. He had had the misfortune to witness tortures and, in all his long life, he had never once known the real truth to come forth as a result of it. He could see the truth being twisted in the mind of the victim as they would say anything if it might stop the agony. He knew too that subjugating people with violence and death was never a solution. Just as if you unfairly wound a man but do not kill him, you will create an enemy for life, so if you unfairly wound a people but do not destroy them completely you will make an enemy for generations.

His own people had done exactly that. When the Romani were just a small city, pushing outwards and exerting influence over the surrounding tribes, they had come up against a large army consisting of several Keltoi tribes, mainly Senones, led by Brennus. Their arrogance saw them insult the leaders of that army, and the resulting battle at the river Allia was a rout. The Senones then continued on to Rome itself and exacted a huge tribute of gold from the Romani. Brennus had sat on one side of a huge set of scales, while gold was piled on the other side. When the Roman leaders had complained that the scales were unfairly fixed, the Senones had thrown swords and armour on and their leader declared loudly, "Vai victis!" (woe to the vanquished).

That was almost 400 winters ago, Kaito reflected, and all that time the Romani had been nursing a festering sore. The wound was opened again in Kaito's lifetime when an entire nation had been forced to leave their home. The land of the Cimbri, where he was now, had been inundated with rising waters. Huge areas of what had been land were now seas or lakes, and the farms and villages that had been there were abandoned. Almost an entire nation had left and roamed around the continent through Gallic lands where they were repulsed or forced to move on until, in time, they clashed with the Roman legions. Those battles had seen the Romani utterly destroyed in the field, and yet the city had found new legions and a new leader. Marius had forced even the poorest men who owned no land at all to join up and, by some level of cunning that suggested the Gods had assisted him, he defeated the Cimbri and destroyed them entirely. Scarcely a single man, woman or child had escaped, and all those who survived the battle became slaves.

The great difference between the Romani and the Keltoi, as Kaito saw it, was that the Keltoi had left people alive after winning their battles, leaving the Romani to rebuild and return to exact revenge, but the Romani had destroyed everything, leaving no-one left alive to strike back.

Kaito wondered, however, if the Senones had not continued to Rome, had not burned their houses and stolen and destroyed great works of art, had they not exacted such a great tribute from them and added insult to injury when the consul had complained about the scales, had they not loaded the scales still more, and declared 'woe to the vanquished', would the Romani have developed such a terrible mistrust and hatred of the Keltoi? Kaito sighed loudly so the fisherman turned in surprise, but he was not the type to ask questions and Kaito was left alone with his thoughts.

20

In Capua, Epona had once again joined with Gwenn in listening to the problems of the sick who, for whatever reason, would not or could not make use of a 'proper' Roman physician. They saw poorer patients, who paid with difficulty, sometimes not with money but with produce or treasured family heirlooms. There were some on whom the best medical minds had given up, and still others who just didn't trust doctors or perhaps, more to the point, didn't want to draw attention to themselves with those in authority.

The large group of burly men who burst in, swept everything off the table and laid a seriously wounded man down, were clearly of this latter group. They looked like gladiators, although Epona had never been to the games, and Gwenn had only done so once, to rescue Blyth from otherwise certain death. A man who seemed to be acting as the leader pointed a curved sword at Gwenn. He spoke in common Latin with an accent that Gwenn could not place.

"Help my friend: he's lost a lot of blood."

Gwenn, instead of being terrified, moved closer to the tip of the blade. She looked along its length, straight into the man's dark eyes and said, "Put your little mentula away then, and let us do our job."

The gladiator was completely wrong footed by her bravery and crudeness but lowered the sword and stepped back as Epona and Gwenn went to work. The men had already tied bandages tightly over their friend's wounds, which were considerable: a big gash across the right leg and a smaller one on the back. They focussed on the leg wound, which had missed the femoral artery by inches, but was still very deep. The man was white as a sheet.

The bandage was soaked with blood which was seeping through. Gwenn prepared a pad of clean linen and poured boiling water into a silver bowl – the silver had magical properties that helped ward off the evil which would cause wounds to turn green and then black, almost always resulting in death unless the limb was cut off quickly. Epona searched along the shelves for the necessary ingredients.

"The achilleos is to your right," Gwenn called to her, applying pressure to the wound with one hand.

"The what?" Epona looked puzzled.

"Uh, sorry, kwaitarkos," she said, using the name Epona was more familiar with.

"Oh, of course. Got it!"

Epona handed the jar to Gwenn and took over keeping the pressure on the seeping wound. The sooner they could rebandage it the better.

The small consulting room was crowded with gladiators, with more just outside. One now pushed forward to the front.

"Gwenn?"

She looked up, "Titus?"

Her old friend was dressed in the style of a Gallus. She tried to focus on the job, but her mind filled with questions.

"Is this *the* Titus?" Epona enquired.

"Yes," said Gwenn before turning to Titus.

"What in Lugh's name...?"

"Later!" Epona cut in. "We have a job to do first."

Epona removed the bandage and held the gaping edges of the cut together as Gwenn expertly and ruthlessly cleaned the wound with the hot water, and then pressed a poultice of the herbs on and tied the bandage into place.

"Can you drink?" she asked the patient, who was woozy but conscious.

"Opimian?" he asked, with a rueful grin.

There was a ripple of nervous laughter from the men.

"Not quite such a fine vintage. In fact, I doubt the local taberna would give this away but, if you drink it all, you might live long enough to enjoy a half decent Falernian one day."

She handed him the cup, and he downed it in a single gulp, pulling a face which indicated Gwenn had not exaggerated its dubious qualities. He said something very crude in a Gallic language. Epona replied in the same language. It was clear, from those who laughed, which of the group spoke the language and which did not.

The ladies helped their patient roll over, so they could clean and rebandage the wound on his back.

"Can you walk?" asked the leader of the group.

"I think so," he replied, trying to get up.

"Hold on there; you need to rest." Gwenn put her hand out and pushed him down.

"We have to leave, now," urged the leader. "If he can't walk, we have no choice but to leave him behind."

"No! I'm not going back. Any one of us will be crucified if we are caught. You know that."

"What?" Gwenn looked from the patient, to the leader, to Titus, seeking answers.

Titus was the first to tell her.

"We just broke out from the ludus of Batiatus. I became a gladiator to pay off debts, but the lanista, Gnaeus Cornelius Lentulus Batiatus, is a cruel and evil man, and eventually we hatched a plan to escape. Someone leaked our plan and we had to fight our way out. Boios here was injured in the fight, but not before he killed two of them with a kitchen knife! There's no way back for any of us now. We have to escape from Roman lands completely. I hope to get to Galatia, Boios dreams of finding a tribe in Gaul who will accept him, as do Crixus here, and Oenomaus," he indicated two more of his comrades, "and this is our leader, Spartacus, whose home lies east of here."

Spartacus admitted, "Boios is right. If we can get away peacefully we will. But, if they fight, we fight to the death. There can be no going back. If we surrender, we will be killed, either in the arena, or tied to a post. Whatever happens, it will be more humiliating and painful than death in battle. That's why we have to go now!"

Gwenn looked at Titus, and asked, "Did you run into debts because of helping me when I was in Ostia?"

"Well…" Titus looked down, but Gwenn could see that he was trying to spare her the truth.

"Come on!" she said, grabbing her staff and pack from the back of the shop. Epona did likewise, and some of the men helped Boios to his feet, half carrying him to the door.

21

Kaito knew he had finally caught up with Blyth. It was late evening; in fact a new day was about to begin as Bellenos slipped below the horizon, and the sky had turned from a dull grey to a darkening dusky blue. It was that time when men gave way to wolves as the master hunters of the wilderness and, in a reverse of those traditional roles, the wolf transformed back into the small elderly figure of Kaito, the greatest mage in the world, cloaked in purple with an oak staff.

He approached the small lakeside village and called out when he was close enough for anyone to hear. After a time, a man emerged, and very quickly after him was the unmistakable figure of Blyth who, on catching sight of Kaito, burst into a run to greet him. The young man practically swept his living ancestor off his feet. "Kaito! I'm a father! You're…" there was no convention for saying it in their native language, the concept being unheard of. "You're the great-father of a great-father!"

Kaito's face creased in a thousand places as a huge smile splintered his wind-blown leathery skin. The two men stumped back to the roundhouse. Biarni ushered them inside, Blodwyth fussed about her appearance and checked the baby, while Biarnafa cleared a space for the new guest to be seated and checked the water was on the fire to boil.

"Well? ... Is it a boy or a girl?" Kaito asked.

"A boy," Blyth confirmed.

Kaito's expression gave no clue as to his feelings either way.

"Does he have a name?"

"We thought Kallon?"

"You don't have to ask my permission."

After Kaito had held Kallon - briefly, as he was not one for cooing over scarcely formed humans - and had enjoyed their host's hospitality, he and Blyth went for a walk to allow them to speak freely. They left Blodwyth feeding Kallon and wrapped their cloaks around them against the cold dark night. Blyth spoke first, his breath curling in smoky wisps in the cold air. He was burning to understand something that had burdened him for many years. A burden which, even now, outweighed his own awful descent into the abyss of his own mind.

"I don't understand how it happened. My father dying, I mean. You warned us there was a storm coming, all those years ago, and we just thought you were mistaken or..." He paused, not wanting to admit they had thought that Kaito was just a crazy old man.

Then he went on, "Anyway, then, just as it all seemed as though everything was going to be perfect, with our father home at last, I thought... Well, I don't really know what I thought, but I felt hopeful. There was a storm of course, a terrible storm, as you know only too well. But I certainly never once imagined that everything would fall apart so completely."

Blyth look sullen and subdued for a moment before he spoke again. "I saw him. My father, I mean. I saw his face lit up by the lightning. He looked... Happy is not the right word; I don't know if there is a word to describe how he looked. It was... as though... he could already see the great feasting hall of Lugh, as though he were already there, walking through the great doors out of the darkness and into the brilliant light and the warmth inside. And the rain was lashing down, and they threw him face down in the swamp, and they killed him. They killed my father, and then later I learned that he possessed magical powers; I've learned to use those powers myself. Darruwen did not possess such power, did he?"

"He did not."

"Then why in the name of all the Gods did my father not simply bat him away? He could have destroyed Darruwen with a wave of his staff: without it, even! It doesn't make any sense. Do you know what went wrong? Why is my father dead? Why is your grandson dead? Why is Trethiwr dead?"

22

Kaito listened to Blyth and then he spoke.

"Your father was a brilliant but a troubled man. He was blessed with a gift from the Gods: a gift beyond price. But the Gods took their fee, as Gods will. In his all too short life he travelled further and saw more wonders than any man should have the right to. His powers were among the greatest of any man who has ever lived, perhaps of any man who is yet to live? I don't know, for there are many men who will come after him, and perhaps the Gods will seek to bestow their powers on others, generations from now. It matters not as we will be long gone by then. But, even if the Gods seek to endow another man with gifts such as Trethiwr possessed, I hope they are never so capricious also as to exact such a price, although… Regrettably, I think my hope is already in vain." Kaito glanced momentarily at Blyth and sighed, his breath curling into abstract shapes against the moonlit sky.

"Trethiwr was cursed with a love so deep for the Gods that he seemed to spend as much effort trying to join them as he did enjoying the life he already had. You have heard that he once tried to swim to the land of Lugh, from Ynys-Manaw?"

Blyth nodded, remembering how he had attempted to swim after the ships that had taken his beloved Blodwyth away.

Kaito continued, "Well, disregarding the fact that Eiru is in his path, no man could swim that far. The cold of the sea would sap his strength long before he made it much beyond sight of shore. When your father was pulled out of the waters he was blue; the sailors wrapped him in the warmest things they could find, and they poured warmed water and honey down his throat, because the cold gets you from inside as well as out at the same time. He kept babbling at them to let him go back. When he knew that they would not, he cried. He wept for some time and rocked back and forth like a small child in his mother's lap. The fishermen were at a loss and were glad to hand him over to the Deru-Weidi of the oak groves and get back to their trade.

"The elders confined him to a hut with a guard, though in truth not one of them could hold him against his will, even by then. Indeed, just as you yourself have learned, powers such as we enjoy are not normal even among the wise oak mages. The oak staff is just for show and ceremonies. Our power lies in secret knowledge, psychology, and the people's belief in the Gods. Why do we spend twenty years teaching the uses of every plant and how it can be used in food, in medicine, and rituals? Why do we make young men and women memorise and recite all the histories of our people? Why do we show our acolytes how to make smoke appear from nothing, or how to make things disappear and reappear with just a wave of the hand? Why do we make sure they know the law, not just the law of their own tribe, but of every tribe, and we teach them the old laws which no longer apply, and we teach them the fundamental laws of the Gods, above all others, the laws that apply even when there is no law that can apply to you?"

Blyth knew that Kaito was not seeking answers to these questions, but he was itching to answer nevertheless, however Kaito ploughed on.

"Most Deru-Weidi have no powers save those that we teach them. You and your brothers are rare indeed. The sons of two mages with true magic. Your mother is the daughter of an Iceni Deru-Weida and, as you know, she has the power to transform into a horse and more besides; though she usually confines herself to a curse, or a little boost to her already considerable charm, I understand.

But Trethiwr? Trethiwr could send forth fire from his staff, not just a spark to light a fire quickly, either. No, I am talking of a ball of flames like that which a dragon produces. He could twist the winds to do his bidding, raise up the seas - or calm them - with a wave of his hands. He could shake the earth and open it up, call the creatures of the forest to his will, heal the dying even as their last drop of life's blood was seeping into the dirt, call upon the denizens of the underworld in black shapeless forms to hold back his enemies, but he could not control the demons in his own head.

There were times when he was unable to move from his bed, for fear of the hatred he 'knew' the world held for him. Before Epona knew him, I spent many nights sitting with him while he refused to leave the safety of his furs. At those times, he never tried to hurt any living thing, neither me, nor the hare which often served as his only comfort. No, he never hurt any living thing because it was himself he hated, and himself he hurt - more often by omission. He failed to eat for days and had to have water forced between his lips. He lost weight at that time; I hope you never see a man waste away so badly. But that was not the worst of it. He cut himself, and he poured hot water on his hands. On one occasion, he took poison. There is no question but that he knew what he was doing. Your father did not make mistakes with plants."

Blyth kept his thoughts to himself, but he realised all these revelations sounded painfully familiar.

"At other times he was a tower of strength and the life and soul of the feast. Then, nobody could stop him in his wild schemes and he loved nothing more than a good drink of mead, seemingly able to outdrink even the strongest warrior, in his youth of course. Then on his travels he visited the place known as the 'Red Lands'. The Romani and the Helleni call it Aegyptus. He went further, down beyond the lands of Kush and into the greatest deepest forest there is. There he met people who lived in the trees."

"Dryads?"

"I don't believe so. My understanding is they were people just like us, but mostly shorter in stature, their skin the colour of a ripe hazelnut, sometimes darker; and they lived in the trees, or at least among them; deep in the forest. Their knowledge of herbs and plants was different from ours because they had different plants. The forest, so Trethiwr told me, contained more different plants and crawling creatures than one acolyte could memorise in twice twenty years. The sophistication of these people knew no limits. They could make everything they needed from the plants and animals that lived in the forests all around them. They had no need for trade, no need for permanent houses, and certainly no use for kings or chiefs beyond a head man of each family who would protect the women, the elderly and the young with the most powerful warriors in the group to back him up.

"The extended family unit was like a wolf pack, owing no allegiance to any larger pack nor claiming any from a smaller, keeping no stores and living each day for the day. They laughed, they cried, they had babies, and their old died and never once did any record the histories even as stories to hand down and remember, nor did they plan for the future. Unless they were mourning the loss of a family member, or if one was sick and no medicine nor any of their Gods could help, then they were always happy. Happiness was their basic state of being, where ours is worry, or jealousy, or resentment, or anger. The Romans are even worse. That's why their generals always scowl; because they are never happy unless they are looting another tribe's gold or riding in triumph through their city.

"What it must be, to be happy and content all the time. Trethiwr tried to learn from them, but his sadness came from the Gods, and there was no human means to keep it at bay. He told me that when the 'darkness' descends - he always referred to it as the 'darkness' - it would feel as though there was nothing. Not that there was nothing in the world, but that there was nothing inside himself. That he was nothing: as though he had no soul."

Kaito stopped speaking and looked at his great grandson.

23

Blyth shuddered, and his scalp tightened until it felt like his head would cave in. His arms were covered in tiny bumps like the skin of a plucked bird, and he could feel every tiny hair on the back of his neck standing on end. His stomach flipped like a rabbit struck by slingshot. He felt that every word Kaito had just spoken about his own father might just as easily apply to him. But even though he had spoken for a long time and told Blyth a great deal, he had not really answered the question.

"But why did he allow the mage Darruwen to have him killed, and so brutally? Surely he cannot now be with Lugh, since he was left in a stinking swamp with no weapons or jewellery?"

Kaito thought for a long moment before answering. "I understand that Trethiwr saw things differently but, before I try to help you understand what your father did and why, I would like to discuss something separate, but related, if you will indulge an old man?"

Blyth nodded.

Kaito continued, "Let us first remember that, for all we are taught, it is not possible to understand the ways of the Gods. Since the first humans were created, the Gods have become distant. No longer do they walk among us in physical form, but they make their presence known by manifesting in other ways. Bellenos does not ride a chariot of burning fire across the sky as he did in the first days but instead sends his *eikon*, to use a Hellenic word, which means an image that represents him. Similarly, the goddess Epona does not ride forth as a horse, but her spirit can be seen in every horse you see. But since the Gods have withdrawn from our world we cannot ask them questions directly, and so we must try to guess their intentions. We equip our dead warriors with weapons, food, and gold, for use in the next life, but who is to say they are needed? The Romani and the Helleni have similar beliefs although they differ because they believe in different Gods. That alone is a clue to the puzzle for, if the Gods walked among us, then all the tribes would have the same Gods, would they not?"

"I suppose that must be true," admitted Blyth.

"But in the far eastern lands that I travelled to in my youth, the lands of the Han tribe and others, it is widely believed that rather than a straight line from life into afterlife, every living thing goes around in circles. Just as the crops grow and are harvested and then regrow again from seed so too, they say, does every living thing die and then become reborn in a new living thing. They call this cycle Samsāra and the rebirth they call Punarbharva. I spent many years learning from the wisest teachers of this belief, and it has great appeal to me."

He went on, "I wanted you to understand that there are different beliefs about what happens when we die; there are different Gods. Indeed, in some lands, they believe there is just one all-powerful god, and in other lands they do not believe in Gods at all! As such, it can be little surprise when someone as well-travelled and as wise as your father takes a different view from that which prevails among his own people."

Kaito paused, until he sensed that Blyth had absorbed this concept.

"Your father told me that he had already travelled to the lands of the shining one, had feasted in his halls, and gazed upon eternally sunlit meadows overflowing with crops, walked through woods teeming with game, danced with fair maidens to music played by the greatest of bards, and slept on a bed of fourscore furs. When he awoke he was in the deep dark forests, where I told you already that he had travelled, far beyond the lands of Aegyptus. He told me that he intended to return home to see his family, and then he hoped to make the journey to those lands again, this time never to return. I am afraid that I perhaps did not take him seriously, or misjudged his plans, and failed to prevent his death. But perhaps I would have had no right to interfere if it was truly his wish to die as he did."

"But why would he choose to die such a terrible death? I think he had been forced to drink a potion with mistletoe that would have made the pain all the more potent."

"This is the key; he had somehow become convinced that his life in this realm was of no importance and that it was merely preparation for the world after this life. His vision of the next realm was far more wonderful than any I have imagined, or any culture I know of. Whether these ideas grew from his own mind, or from some culture he came into contact with, I cannot say. But he believed that the afterlife was, in a sense, the *real* life, while this one that we experience now is just a shadow of it.

"More importantly, he was convinced that he must die a painful death bravely, rather than a peaceful death, in order to reach that world. But, as one who disdained arms and fighting, there was little prospect of that happening, unless he made it happen himself. If you remember also that he was cursed by the Gods with extremes of temperament, from being exuberant and productive at one time, to being like a hollowed-out shell filled with darkness at another, then even allowing that he had learned ways to control that darkness, the combination of his beliefs and that curse must have been enough to tip him over the edge. I do hope he reached the realm which he so fervently believed in, but that we may never know."

24

Blyth had listened intently to every word, and he felt the need to unburden himself of his own problems. He opened his mouth to speak and it came out as a hoarse croak, "I've had that feeling."

He adjusted himself and spoke more clearly at the second attempt. "I have felt like that, exactly like my father: the feeling of complete emptiness, like the void before time began, like Khaos."

Kaito waited patiently, not interrupting but watching the young man with interest and compassion. He knew. He had probably always known. The same curse had been handed to almost every generation of his line, along with great magical power, and each generation had to learn to deal with it anew as none had ever really found a way to conquer it.

Blyth went on. "I thought I was sad because Blodwyth had been taken from me, but that does not make sense. When she was taken I was angry and foolish, but not empty. I realise I have had moments when I felt down for no good reason before, but this last time it was beyond imagining, and yet I was getting close to catching up with Blodwyth when it struck. I boarded a ship, and it was as though clouds descended and enveloped me. I can't remember much but then I woke up in the house of a mage who looks a little like my mother, although I think I mistook her for someone else, and I already felt much better; more alive, more… real than I had felt for days. I don't ever want to feel like that again. I'd rather die. I can honestly believe… if my father thought he was going to feel like that again… or if he was already feeling like that, then… then even a terrible death would seem like a mercy. It all makes sense now.

Kaito spoke softly, "I've lost a son and a grandson. I would prefer it if you could outlive me, please?"

"I'm sorry, Kaito. The Gods have treated you harshly."

"Perhaps. But in my long life I have seen people rise to power who then end their life in horrific agony. And I am hardly the only father to lose a son. I once knew of a family who had seven children, and not one of them lived beyond their fifth Samhain. Sometimes, the Gods seem to draw straws, or roll bones, to decide who lives and who dies; to decide who will win the battle and who must take hemlock or fall upon the mercy of the victor. In a way, and on a purely personal level, the Gods have been unusually kind to me."

Blyth nodded imperceptibly, then Kaito said, "I am old, and my bones feel the cold; let's go inside and warm up before you end up having to build me a pyre."

"One last question, if I may?" Blyth began.

"Go on," Kaito said, hesitating as he turned to go inside.

"Why were you not the chief at Ba-Dun, instead of Urien?"

"Because Urien persuaded the elders that he would make the better chief."

"But you possess powerful magic. You could have destroyed him or forced the people to choose you."

"And rule by force of magic alone? How long do you suppose I could maintain such a scheme?"

"But…"

"When you wield magic, are you not tired afterwards?"

Blyth shrugged and grunted his unwilling acknowledgement of the truth of this.

"If you take power with sword and spear, you must hold onto it with sword and spear. If you take power with words, you must hold onto it with words. And it follows that if you take power with magic, then you must…?"

"Hold onto it with magic?" Blyth finished.

"Exactly! And how long could you sustain continual use of magic?"

"Scarcely from sunset to sunrise," Blyth admitted, knowing that even that would be too long for continuous magic.

"Of course, you would not need to use it all the time. Merely every time there was any challenge to your authority. It is enough to ensure that we prefer to work on the edges of power, to assist those with the words and the swords to make the decisions and take on the role of leadership, while we advise them.

"You know the Deru-Weidi wield the true power because the people believe that we can remove them from the Gods. We, and only we, have the power to cut them off from religious rites and festivals. Only we can cast them out into the wilderness, to scavenge for food. Only we can take away the protection of the law so that, should any man hurt them, they have no recourse. We do all that without the need even for true magic. But to rule outright, with magic, is too much even for me.

"I tried to become the chief because I wanted to unite all the tribes peacefully for the good of all, but Urien persuaded the elders that we should instead seek to take over by force and I decided I had had enough of other people completely. I sought solitude and inner peace for my own good. Perhaps that was a mistake; which man can say that he knows everything and always makes the right choice? If any, then he is a liar.

"I fear that our lack of unity will be our undoing; perhaps not in my lifetime, but there will come a time when the Romani become strong enough to send their legions to our shores. When they come, they will not respect our ways. They fear the Deru-Weidi because we do not bow to other Gods and because we are the only uniting force among all the hundreds of tribes and clans. They will seek to destroy us before anything else, and then our magic will only help to slow them down or help us to hide from them.

"You and I, your brothers, and Elarch, are the most powerful of any Deru-Weidi I know. There are others such as Gwenn, Llwyd, Alisa, Telamonos, and Dwbrana, more yet at Lugh-Dun, and others scattered around the tribes, but none with half as much magic as you or I and most of our power is for healing not warfare. It really is getting very cold!"

"I am sorry, Kaito. Let's get inside to warm by the fire." Blyth gently put his hand on Kaito's back as they both walked back to the house, a thousand thoughts jostling for attention in his mind.

25

The view from the top of Vesuvius was breathtaking and somewhat surreal. The vast expanse of countryside stretching out before them, the neat rows of vines, dark and sombre, hugging the slopes, the bright yellow of ripening wheat on the plains lower down, and wooded areas dotted in between resembled the Elysian fields or the land where Lugh held court among the dead souls of the bravest warriors. In the other direction they looked down into an abyss which seemed like Tartarus brought to Earth. Older men recalled stories from their childhood, told by their grandparents, of when this mountain had belched forth fires and burning rocks, though the stories were not generally believed by the younger generation. Certainly not by the farmers who planted crops right on the slopes almost to the rim of the crater where they stood now. The soil was renowned as being among the richest and most fertile in Italia, and the wines produced here were famous in all the known world. Gwenn pondered recent events as she tried to make sense of everything that had happened as well as that which seemed about to unfold.

Men of the Wise Oak

The route by which they had arrived here had been astonishing. When the gladiators had broken out from the ludus there was little more on their minds than escaping the cruel lanista. Having escaped, their next thought had been simply to get as far away from Capua as possible and eventually away from Rome altogether. These men had burst into the little taberna where Gwenn and Epona dispensed medical aid to those who, for whatever reason, chose not to see a 'proper' Roman or Greek medicus. After helping their wounded comrade, the ladies had joined them partly to help their latest patient, to whom they felt they owed a duty of care, but also because Gwenn felt that she owed her old friend Titus assistance, since she felt that her actions had led him into his current predicament.

The party of escaped gladiators, now bringing a wounded man with them and joined by two females, escaped the city itself and now had to make their way through the surrounding countryside. Naturally their next concern had been the need to obtain food and water. Raiding a farm had been easy, made all the easier when the agricultural slaves took the opportunity to revolt against their masters and join the gladiators.

Household slaves were usually loyal to their masters and in return would enjoy a certain amount of comfort and consideration. Often there were opportunities to make a little money for themselves; some were even able to buy their freedom. Others could look forward to being freed as part of their master's will. However, those who were found to be unsatisfactory, or rebellious, assuming their sins were not so serious as to be punishable by crucifixion, would be sold off as inferior goods. These would then find themselves doing much harder work on farms, in mines, or loading ships in port. These slaves had no personal connection with their masters who kept hundreds, sometimes thousands, of slaves. With no possibility of manumission, or any other sign of hope, these slaves saw the gladiators as a beacon of hope and began to join them in increasing numbers. The larger the party grew, the more farms it had to raid, and the more slaves joined them.

A militia was sent out from Capua and were soundly defeated by the slaves who, it turned out, were not quite the rabble that the soldiers had expected them to be. Since most had previously been warriors who had been captured when their lands had been taken by the Romans, they had both the skills and the bitter hatred of their captors which gave them strength, even despite using makeshift weapons such as agricultural tools. Having defeated their first real opposition, they also now had considerably more weapons and armour than previously, and now they began to organise themselves into cohorts and to choose leaders.

The obvious candidates for leadership were among those who had broken out originally, and so command fell to two of the Gauls, Crixus and Oenomaus, and to Spartacus, the Thracian who had thrust his sword at Gwenn when they brought their wounded comrade in. Just as she had been drawn to Caesar, she was now also drawn to the charismatic and effective leadership of

Spartacus. For his part, he had admired her courage in the face of his sword, and now also found her to be a good listener with an astonishing grasp of tactics. She quickly became the equivalent of his personal tribune.

Each time the authorities sent any kind of force to deal with the slaves, the slaves gained more arms and armour, while Campanians and Romans lay dead in the field. Eventually, however, a much larger force was sent from Rome itself. On the edges of their growing army there was a network of locals with connections. By now many of their number were not slaves, but free men who had witnessed, and deplored, the way Rome treated their allies in the earlier social wars. Campania was an old region with its own customs and history, unrelated to Rome. Cities like Capua, Herculaneum and Pompeii were at least as old as Rome and just as proud. Bitterness fuelled the minds of men who pulled out their armour and gladius from storage and joined Spartacus and the slave army. News fed through that a much larger force was coming from Rome, led by one of that year's praetors, Gaius Claudius Glaber. Nobody had heard of him or knew anything of his skills, or otherwise, as a general. Nevertheless, if Roman legions were on their way, the slaves would face their toughest challenge yet.

26

Spartacus was angry as he had not been since before their escape. "I need to know more about what we will face!" he stormed. Crixus and Oenomaus were there of course. Crixus did most of the talking.

"All we know is he is a praetor, from a plebeian family, and that he is collecting men on his way to here."

"Not a proper legion then. Only militia, just as we have already faced and swept aside like mosquitoes." Spartacus smiled a terrifying grin.

"A larger force however, or so I understand." Crixus interjected with a note of caution.

"How large? Has anyone seen them yet?"

"Not directly, yet."

"As soon as someone does I need an estimate of numbers."

"It goes without saying, I assure you."

"We will continue to drill the men then until we know more. If we are to fight against Romans, then we must at least learn how to fight like Romans. I don't mind ambushing them, or getting behind their lines if we can, but if it comes to a straight battle, I don't want any individual heroics, such as you Gauls are so fond of."

"You'll hear no objection to that from either of us," Oenomaus put in. We've been around Romans long enough to know that pitched battles are not won by individuals."

Outside, it was clear that Oenomaus was speaking the truth. The three leaders had appointed centurions, there being now well over a thousand men in their ranks. These had, in turn, appointed other positions, and now lines of men were being drilled to keep their shields locked and stab with a sword or spear, not to break ranks and slash wildly as some might have done in the heat of battle. The shields were not all properly matched, but the centurions had made sure the front ranks had the best and most suitable shields for the job. With luck, and discipline, they would not need to use the least able and least well-equipped men at all.

Then the first observer reports arrived that Glaber commanded an army of some three thousand fully armed militia. A ripple of fear and adrenaline passed around the slaves' camp as word got out. As Glaber advanced, Spartacus moved his smaller and less well armed force away in search of favourable ground. Both he and the two Gaulish commanders knew they were delaying the inevitable. In a straight clash, a rag-tag bunch of angry slaves and farmers, led by a few gladiators, stood little chance against a trained militia led by a Roman praetor. The only question might be how long would the losers survive tied to a cross in the heat of the sun. When they made their stand, Spartacus wanted to be quite sure he would die by a sword or spear, and not of thirst with his arms slowly being dragged from their sockets by his own bodyweight. He led his men in the only direction that seemed available: up the slopes of Vesuvius, through vineyards where they took whatever wine they could find.

"We may as well die drunk," Spartacus laughed mirthlessly. "Hey Boios! It's not Opimian, not even Falernian I'm sorry to say." He passed a jug to the injured gladiator who was by now at least fully mobile and reasonably well recovered.

He took a swig, and almost instantly sprayed the wine out. "Ugh, is that wine? Tastes more like garum!"

Gwenn and Epona were still with them. Not only had Gwenn formed a mutual bond with Spartacus, but Epona had been drawn to Crixus in a more physical way, and the feeling was mutual despite Epona's greater age. There was also a strange fascination about what was happening and neither woman wanted to miss what was going on. Although the prospect of being caught in the midst of battle was not appealing, they did at least have unique ways of getting out of trouble. They were not the only women in the growing army, as there had been a number of female slaves who they felt they could not leave behind, and a few free women had joined their husbands rather than remain behind on an abandoned farm.

Gwenn took a sip from the wine jug, "It's not so bad, but it hasn't aged well."

She passed it to Epona. "I've had better," Epona agreed, "but if you don't like this, then I'm not sure you would appreciate a good Falernian anyway."

They moved on up the slope, aware that Glaber was not far behind and that he was unlikely to stop for a wine tasting session any time soon. Eventually, and inevitably, they found themselves at the top of the mountain, a long wide rocky rim encircling a wide shallow bowl of barren rock with a further small conical peak near the middle, barely rising above the rim. This area was overgrown with scrub, surrounded by arcadian perfection. Below them, on the route they had taken to get there, were ranged some three thousand fully armed men led by the praetor Gaius Claudius Glaber. Not a legion it was true, but nevertheless their ranks would have been filled with many well-trained soldiers.

Scouts had already assessed their options. The area was bleak and their prospects against Glaber's army in a pitched battle were bleaker still. There were no farms here, of course, and therefore no source of food, nor of water. There was vegetation here, but scarcely enough to sustain an army. Gwenn and Epona could have survived on this mountainside indefinitely, subsisting on nettles and other wild plants, which grew in profusion anywhere where there was adequate soil, but for a large force like this they had enough to last a few days at most. There was also, despite all their confident expectations, no safe route down the mountainside other than that by which they had come. This fact greatly surprised the leaders, who had all seen the mountain from a distance and noted its roughly conical shape. None had, however, noted the remarkably steep sides near the top, nor realised how soft and breakable the rock was. Climbing down the almost vertical cliff walls would have been easy for a spider, or for one of the little geckos, which flitted among the rocks and disappeared into crevices when disturbed, but was out of the question for any but the most agile and fit human, and even then only if he or she was unencumbered by weapons or provisions of any kind.

The alternative was to head back down the mountain and engage Glaber's forces in a pitched battle. This was exactly what Glaber wanted and had prepared for. His camp, and his three thousand men, were spread out only so far as was needed to cut off all escape, and they were dug in so as to provide the maximum obstacle to any frontal assault. Spartacus would have expected nothing less. A legion of nearly six thousand men including auxiliaries could dig a trench a mile long and twelve feet deep in the space of a few hours and have the soil built up into a wall behind it in the same time. They were trapped, and Spartacus knew it. So did Crixus, and Oenomaus. And if the leaders knew it, the men would not be far behind. Most of the original gladiators who had escaped were present for the deliberations, as were Gwenn and Epona, although they were probably not expected to contribute their opinions.

Crixus was all for decisive action. "I say we attack them. It's all or nothing."

"Then it is nothing, but we have nothing else," Spartacus said with resigned calmness.

"Shall we give the orders to prepare for battle then?" Oenomaus asked.

"I would prefer to hear an alternative; if anyone has any ideas, now's the time to voice them."

"I have a suggestion," Gwenn began. The men looked at her and, since none said anything to prevent her, she went on.

"I know how we can get off the mountain safely without facing Glaber."

There was silence until eventually Spartacus said, "Do continue."

"We can make ropes from plants growing here."

Epona gasped in realisation of the truth of this, "Gwenn! Why didn't I think of that?"

"You would have soon enough," Gwenn said, generously.

"Ropes?" Crixus queried. "Is there time?"

"There is if everyone helps, and there is no shortage of materials growing everywhere you look."

27

Soon, Gwenn and Epona had shown some of the men and women which plants to collect, and the best method of doing so. Then they moved on to showing others how to prepare the plants to keep the best lengths of the long tough fibres that would be needed. They needed a considerable length of rope thick enough to take the weight of a fully armed man, and they needed several, otherwise it would take days to get everyone off the mountain one at a time.

Many individuals stepped up and revealed they were familiar with one or more parts of the process. Lots of them had made snares for hunting using plant fibres; these were farming people after all. Luckier still, some had been sailors or fishermen and were skilled rope-makers. With everyone designated jobs to do, the upper slopes of the mountain were swiftly denuded of the best plants for rope-making. Heaps of unwanted pith were mounding up while lengths of thin cord were being fed into the final process of rope making.

By the evening of the next day, to the astonishment of everyone, even Gwenn, they were ready with a dozen ropes long enough to send men and materials down the cliffs.

"If we start now, it will be after sunset by the time we get everyone down, and we can slip away under cover of darkness," Gwenn suggested.

"Better yet, if we sleep now, and start before dawn, we can attack their camp from the rear," Crixus suggested.

"I agree," Oenomaus said. "If we run they will only follow, and we must face them again on another day. Better to attack them on our terms and finish them off."

"And then they will send more and larger forces, whole legions or many legions," Gwenn countered. She thought of Gaius Julius Caesar who had been captured by pirates. When he had raised the ransom to buy his freedom, he had promised them he would return to capture them and that he would see them all crucified. They had laughed, but Caesar had done exactly as he had promised. She remembered the sight of hundreds of men tied up to posts sunk into the ground. Caesar had shown them mercy and slit their throats, but yet they hung there for all to see while their corpses rotted. It sent a chill through her to think of it. She wondered then, had Caesar failed to find the pirates as easily as he had, how long would he have continued his search. How much trouble would he have gone to in order to fulfil his promise to crucify every last man among them. She suspected that he would have succeeded, or died trying, no matter how long it took.

Spartacus mused, "I agree with Crixus and Oenomaus. We will have to face them sooner or later. Better on our terms. And if they send legions we must fight them too but always, if we can, on our terms. As much as we may drill the men, we will always fight best when they cannot form ranks against us."

He raised his voice for the masses of men to hear. "We are not fleeing, men. We will sleep now, and before dawn we will descend these ropes. When we reach the bottom, we will regroup and attack Glaber from behind, where his defences are weakest."

There was a cheer from the men, none of whom were in the mood for sneaking away in the night anyway. Most slept, a few could not. Before dawn they woke their comrades and then one by one the men began to climb down the ropes that had been set up. It was a terrifying prospect for the first men to go in almost complete darkness. They had to trust in the strength of an untested rope, tied to a stunted tree. One rope did indeed slip from its mooring, neither the tree nor the rope had failed but the knot itself. The man who tied it was at the bottom of the cliff, presumably a mangled corpse. Most got down safely, and those who followed had the sound of voices below as well as the moonlight to guide them. Leaning back against the rock and walking down hand over hand was the safest way, but many struggled with this, and panicked, and only ended up reaching the bottom safely out of a sheer bloody-minded determination not to die. One or two failed even in that respect, losing their grip and plummeting to the bottom. Most had managed to get nearly all the way down and suffered only superficial injuries though.

Supplies also had to be lowered. Gwenn and Epona, still on the summit, took personal charge of this operation with a small group of the strongest men who took it in turns to lower the heavy packs on the ropes. Occasionally the ropes broke; they had been very hastily created and could not be expected to last long. Despite the few mishaps however, the vast majority of the men and supplies made it to the safety of the lower slopes unscathed and the men regrouped around their centurions.

"I've sent two men ahead to find their camp," Spartacus explained. "When they report back, we will attack before the sun rises if possible. All torches are to be extinguished; no man is to use any form of artificial light. When we attack we will have the advantage of good vision while their eyes will be accustomed to their campfires."

The orders were passed around as the last few remaining men descended the ropes. There was only one rope remaining which had not given way by now.

"Is everyone down?" Spartacus asked.

Another man was descending one of the few remaining ropes. Evidently it snapped near the top while he was still a few feet from the ground, but he was unharmed as the greenish-brown rope snaked down around him. He got to his feet and answered the Thracian.

"I was the last on this one, thank the Gods. There are just the two Galli women with the last of the provisions up there as far as I know. They insisted I go on and they would finish up," he said.

Nearby a heavy box crashed to the ground and rolled a few paces down the slope before breaking open and disgorging its contents. The rope to which it was tied fell down around it.

"That was the last of the ropes that they were using for the supplies," he said. "That means they are left up there on their own."

Spartacus looked grave, then said, "I've only known those two for a few days but if I have learned anything about them, it is that they can look after themselves. We have a different job to do."

.

28

With the report back from the scouts they were ready to attack. The slave army formed up and moved quietly in the darkness towards the rear of the Roman encampment. As the skies turned the milky blue of predawn they struck. Many throats were cut before any alarm was raised. Men were skewered in their beds, tents set ablaze, those who did manage to get prepared faced an unknown number of ferocious attackers already well prepared and psyched up for battle. Nevertheless, some began to form ranks and give as good as they were getting.

Spartacus, for all his talk of not wanting individual heroics, was drawn from one kill to the next. His gladiatorial training made him a fearsome adversary, hacking down men one after another, and parrying blows with shield and sword with equal skill. He had retained his curved sword, rather than adopt a gladius, making him ill-suited to the thrust and stab of a tight formation anyway. As each new quarry drew him deeper in and further from his own men, he eventually found himself surrounded by an enemy who were facing a crushing defeat but were keen to do as much damage to their foe as they could. Spartacus narrowly dodged the point of one spear and slashed down with his sword, cutting through the wooden shaft. Another spear glanced off his shield, and a third struck his greaves. He parried and slashed with furious energy, but it would surely only be a matter of time before a spear or gladius tip found a gap in his defences. He could not face in every direction at once. Why had he strayed so far from the rest of his men?

He looked around for a friendly face and was astonished to see a woman with long flowing hair, so blonde it was almost white. She was wielding a long sword, of the style favoured by the Gauls, with a rounded tip. It was only of use for slashing and this she did with terrible consequences. Time seemed to slow down for Spartacus as he watched Gwenn's sword sweep down and across, low down. The men before her crumpled and lay still. As time came rushing back, Spartacus instinctively turned to see what other terrors lurked behind him. His sword followed his gaze as he struck again at more attackers and then Gwenn was beside him slashing with devastating effect. She wore no armour, nor even carried a shield. He was astonished, but nevertheless, he was glad she was on their side.

"How did you get away?" he yelled at her.

"I'll tell you later," she lied, as another line of Romans came towards them behind a line of shields.

There was a slope behind them, which fell away steeply for some distance, so they had no option but to stand and fight or jump and take a risk of suffering serious injury.

"What happened to Epona?"

"How do you find enough breath to talk *and* fight?" she asked.

"Good training." He grinned. "Is she alright?"

"She's fine."

The line of militiamen was closing on them, in tight formation. They were unhelmed but that was little consolation to Gwenn or Spartacus armed with sword and shield. They would need ranged weapons and enough space to deploy them to take advantage of the exposed heads. This was how the Romans won battles, not by breaking ranks, but by pushing forward in tight formation, thrusting with the scutum and stabbing with the gladius. Gwenn and Spartacus needed help, but the main battle was going on some distance away and, although it was all going their way, there was no guarantee that help would arrive in time.

Gwenn's sword made contact with a scutum first, and Spartacus' did so immediately afterwards. Neither sword did serious damage to the tough wood of the shield. Spartacus looked behind them briefly.

"Shall we jump?" he asked.

"Hold firm," Gwenn said through gritted teeth as her sword clunked against the tough wood of the scutum again and a gladius poked inches short of her midriff.

There was a peculiar whistling sound, then one of the men crumpled without warning leaving a break in the line. They closed ranks quickly, but another ethereal whistle and another legionary collapsed beside the first. Spartacus was able to see, the second time, that a stone had hit the man in the head. He looked around to see where it had come from, but Gwenn focussed her energy on the next man, who crumpled in a heap seemingly without her sword even damaging his armour. Spartacus assumed that he had also been hit by a stone but didn't have time to consider this. Instead he concentrated on the immediate problem in front of him. He swung his curved sword around the nearest shield, the gap having opened up in the line. The soldier staggered as much from the force of the blow as with the blade which barely cut through the armour. Then another whistle, and another stone hit the next man in the line, and everything was opened up.

Spartacus was grateful to the unseen slinger, but he was concerned that their last shot had required pin-point accuracy to avoid hitting him. As he ploughed into the remaining line, taking them one after another and dispatching each with the ease of a trained gladiator, he was pleased that no more stones seemed to be coming his way. Behind him, when he dared to glance back, Gwenn seemed to be coping with the other end of the line with similar ease. With the last of his quota laying immobile he turned to see her finish off her last adversary. From his viewpoint it was hard to be certain, but it looked as though her sword never touched him, yet the man collapsed as though he had been cut in two. He had not heard any whistling sound but he wondered if the mystery slinger had been involved. Gwenn was exhausted, nonetheless. She had fought hard, even if she had been aided by the slinger.

When all the fighting seemed to be over, Epona appeared walking jauntily and seemingly without a hair out of place.

"Nice of you to show up at last, now the battle is more or less over," Spartacus began, but then he noticed the sling dangling from her right hand and the bag of stones at her waist. "Oh! Was that you with the sling?"

She smiled, but then frowned and dashed over to Gwenn who was still breathing heavily and doubled over. Spartacus joined them.

"You fight well, for a woman," he told Gwenn, in a jovial way. He was rewarded with a glare from Gwenn and a punch on the arm from the diminutive Epona which, nevertheless, hurt more than all the knocks he had received in the battle.

He laughed, "Alright, I'm sorry. You fight well, without qualification. And you..." he looked at Epona. "So that was you with the sling?"

"Yes."

"You took out, how many, six? Seven?"

"Four."

"It was seven," Gwenn interrupted. "You lost count." She gave Epona a look.

"Yes. Seven. Sorry, you know how we Gauls are with counting."

"There's nothing wrong with your aim though. I'll take prowess in battle over counting skills any day. Come on, there's work to be done, and then wine to drink."

"Let's get the work over with then, so we can enjoy the wine."

There was indeed work to do. There were surprisingly few casualties among the slaves, but Gwenn and Epona set to helping those who were wounded. For some, whose injuries were more serious, there was the kindness of a fatal blow to hasten their death. Most of the men set to collecting weapons and armour from the dead militia. Some counted up the bodies. Spartacus, Crixus and Oenomaus were occupied taking reports from their commanders. There had been a handful of militiamen who had escaped. Estimates varied between twenty and a hundred. Spartacus was annoyed but held nobody to blame. It was fate, and some men would naturally flee a battle if they knew they were losing and saw the chance to escape. Glaber had died honourably, but Spartacus suspected that nobody would remember his name. The Romans did not gladly reward failure.

Gathering firewood for a funeral pyre took a long time, and it was getting dark before it could be lit. They watched the flames engulfing the pile of thousands of bodies, the stench of burning flesh drove them away and they marched almost a mile before they felt they could make camp. The next day they would have to move on again. Soon the news of this victory would reach Rome, and Spartacus knew that what Gwenn had said the day before was true. They would raise a legion, and then more, and they would keep sending men against the slave army until they were defeated. Only by leaving Italia did they have any hope of reaching freedom. Perhaps not even then.

29

Teague and Abbon did not depart immediately after Kaito had left to follow Blyth. Teague wanted to consider his options and he was not prone to making decisions precipitously. In many ways he was as unlike Blyth as it was possible for a brother to be. He was not given to wild swings of mood, and seldom acted in the heat of the moment. It was Teague who would back away from conflict at every opportunity, only turning to fight when every other alternative was closed off to him. If that moment arose, he would become savage and attack swiftly, but then seemingly return to complete tranquillity just as quickly.

Abbon was different again. He was inquisitive, with an irrepressible sense of humour. He had a childish streak that remained with him even now as a young man. An expert climber and a dead shot with a sling, Abbon seemed overflowing with confidence, but it was a confidence borne of familiarity. Fear of the unknown was a powerful factor which held him back. Growing up with two older brothers, he never went anywhere for the first time without one or both of them. Now, and for the first time in his life, he had been asked to go into lands where nobody of his tribe, except possibly his own father, had ever been. He wasn't afraid, just unsure. Certainly he would never have left Ynys-Mona before Teague, nor would he have remained after Teague departed.

Teague naturally waited until the new moon before Imbolc before setting out. He made sacrifices and read the signs. Only when he was fully satisfied that the Gods approved of his plans did he leave. Abbon, of course, went with him.

"You know that we both have to go to different places, don't you?"

"Of course, but for the first part of our journey we must go the same way. Aegyptus is in the east. We can part ways there."

"Agreed. I wonder how Mater is getting on with Gwenn."

"If we travel via Italia we might be able to see them before going on to Aegyptus."

"If we can find them," Teague mused.

"If we can find them? 'Blood kin', remember?"

"Oh, yes. I've never felt it before. Probably because I've never had the need to try."

"Really? I sometimes think I can sense her even here. Sometimes I feel worried for no reason. I just assumed that was because she was in trouble."

"I didn't think it worked like that," Teague said, "I thought you had to focus on them and you could sense which direction to go. Nothing more."

"I don't know, but let's try to find her. We can decide what to do later. Depending on whether we can or not."

"Agreed."

The young men were riding their favourite horses, with spare mounts carrying the supplies. They rode through the forests, on the hard-frozen ground, where reports of bandit activity had been less frequent ever since Kaito's visit. Nevertheless they were vigilant and kept their guard up. At night, when they camped, they drew a ring of protection around them which kept predators, both human and animal, at bay.

Almost a week into their journey, they passed through Dwr-y-tryges territory. They had heard that Urien had moved his household to the larger village of Maywr-Dun. A new chief would be in place at their old village of Ba-Dun, and although they would know many people, they felt they would be very much outsiders now. They also avoided passing too close to Maywr-Dun. They did not blame Urien for their father's death, but they sensed Urien would not trust to that and would sooner see them killed than risk their vengeance. Not that they need fear him. Their powers were more than a match, but neither had any interest in destruction. To them, there was simply no point. It could neither put right the wrongs of the past, nor make for a better future.

They travelled the same route as they had done so many years ago, leaving Kaito's house deep in the forest, when he had told them he had taught them all the magic he could. They crossed the sea to the lands of the Unelli where they had first met Gwenn. She of course was not there, but much was familiar as they rode on down through Gaul. They were welcomed by the village mage at every village, almost to the point of having to refuse hospitality in order not to slow down their journey still further. It took the best part of a full moon cycle before they reached Massalia. Independent of Rome yet also under the protection of the republic, it was the ideal port for Abbon and Teague to buy passage on a ship.

Not all ships sailed to Rome, but most did; or rather, to Ostia: the closest port to the greatest city in the known world. The voyage took a little over a week due to the ship putting into harbour at Aleria for rather longer than usual due to a storm. From Ostia they were able to buy passage on another ship to sail down the coast of Italia to Campania, where they believed Gwenn and their mother would be. The ship was headed for Neapolis where the brothers asked for directions to Capua. When they were told the route they both sensed something was not right. Abbon seemingly had a stronger sense of where their mother was, but by now, even Teague was well aware that she was not located in the direction that had been indicated.

Instead of heading north, they turned south towards Herculaneum, with the huge bulk of Vesuvius looming over them.

30

The success of the slave army attracted many more to their ranks. At every farm they passed they freed more agricultural slaves, arming them until the weapons and armour they had taken from Glaber's militia ran out. Men joined them from Campanian towns and now also there were Samnites joining. All these brought their own armour and weapons, as well as much needed experience. Their numbers now in excess of five thousand men, they heard news of another praetor, Publius Varinius, who was advancing on them. He had a similar sized force of around ten cohorts, the size of a legion, although still only a militia, hastily recruited from towns between Rome and Nola. The confidence of the slaves, under their consistently victorious general, Spartacus, was boosted greatly.

This confidence was boosted still further when they received news that Varinius had split his forces, sending just two thousand men ahead under the command of Lucius Furius. The slave army soundly defeated this much smaller force although they escaped the almost complete slaughter that had been meted out to Glaber. The second, larger, force under Lucius

Cossinius fared even worse than Furius had done. Cossinius died in the battle along with almost all his men. They had however dealt a bitter blow to the slave army. Among the casualties was Oenomaus, killed early on in the battle. There was little left of his body after men had trampled him and spears and swords cut him, but Gwenn carried out a Gallic funeral ceremony for him as best she could.

Publius Varinius retreated with what was left of his militia to lick his wounds while Gwenn and Epona worked tirelessly on the injured of the slave army. Some could not be saved. It was a painful decision, but it had to be made. A comrade would then deliver the coup de grâce, either by thrusting a sword up and under the ribcage into the heart, or by delivering a fierce blow to the skull, to finish them off quickly, rather than leave them to die in agony. Even those who could not be healed enough to return to fighting or working would be a dead weight and their capture would only result in a horrific death at the hands of the Romans. There was no way back for any of them now. No returning to farms, not even for those who were freedmen or citizens.

"What have we got ourselves into?" Gwenn asked as she ground up leaves to extract the astringent antiseptic they contained. She didn't think of it in those terms, but the effect it had was to sting and stop wounds from filling up with the thick greenish yellow puss that, if left, would soon turn the area around the wound black. When that happened there was no saving the unfortunate victim. Sometimes it seemed as though more men died from sickness brought about by non-lethal cuts than on the battlefield itself. If you added in the occasional bout of sickness that engulfed whole armies even before the first spear was thrown, that was certainly true.

Epona's reply drew Gwenn out of her reverie. "We're giving the Romani a taste of their own medicine is how I see it. The way this army is growing we could march on Rome itself."

"Is that what we're doing? I just came along because Spartacus fascinates me, and because I feel I owe a debt to Titus. He's been given command of a cohort now, given a good account of himself in battle, and seems to be well liked. Perhaps the debt is paid now?" Gwenn still seemed unsure.

Epona felt on firmer ground. "How this started is one thing, how it will end is up to us. I want to smash Rome, destroy it so that it can never recover. Crixus feels the same way. Ever since Brennus sacked Rome generations ago, they've held a grudge against the Keltoi, against people like you and me. We've never thought of ourselves as a single people, I know. If you ask an Eceni warrior if he is kin to the Belgae, or the Cimbri, or the Vocontii, he would laugh, and possibly make a joke about having been there once and there was this one girl… But the truth is we are all kin. You only have to listen to the languages as they shift from place to place. You can walk from Ynys-Mona to Lugh-Dun, and right down to Mediolanum and pick up the differences as you go so you can still talk to people. We don't see it, but the Romani do. To them we are all one people, and they want to take their revenge for the last time we burned their city."

"So, you are driven by hatred and revenge?" Gwenn questioned.

"Me? Deus Pater no! It's they who seek revenge. I never set out to do anything but what Kaito asked me which was to make you see sense and end your love affair with these odious people."

"I'm not in love with anybody. I just have the ability to see the good in everybody. Something you should try sometime."

There was venom in Epona's voice as she replied, "Oh I can see the good in them. They have a good deal of pride, they're good at stealing land, and gold, and crops. They are good at telling other people what to do. It's good to see their guts feed the soil. I'll tell you what they are good for: nothing!"

"Did you forget a vow you took once? We're supposed to heal people, not destroy them."

"I'm healing people, aren't I?" Epona said as she slapped a poultice viciously onto a wounded man's leg and tied the bandage as though she were attempting to strangle a kitten. "Anyway," she added," I didn't see you healing any of those Romani militia earlier. Unless decapitating someone is a new kind of medicine?"

"If it is me or them, I would sooner it be them," was all Gwenn said in reply. She would leave Epona to let off steam, as she obviously needed to, rather than fight back and make matters worse.

The smaller but more fiery woman did indeed continue at length about the many faults of the Romans, and how much better were her people, and for all that she had talked about the hundreds of different tribes being one people, she now referred only to her own Eceni, and to the Dwr-Y-Tryges into which she had been tied by the bond between her and Trethiwr. She was silenced completely however, when two young men appeared and, after a moment, she recognised them as her own sons.

There was an emotional greeting, and then Epona roped them into helping with the wounded. Fortunately both had learned well at Ynys-Mona and were able to assist Gwenn and their mother as though they had been doing so for years.

They talked and answered an endless stream of questions as they worked and told the two women what they were doing, where they were going, and why. They explained that they had decided to find Epona and catch up before carrying on their way, first to Aegyptus and then parting ways heading for their respective goals. They even confessed they had wagered a gold torc on which would return first.

It was late before anyone was allowed to relax; while Gwenn and Epona worked on the sick, the main job was, as always, collecting any weapons and armour, and preparing fires to burn the bodies. They were able to find a large quantity of aromatic oil which was added to the pyre which helped greatly with the stench of burning flesh.

31

Spartacus went around the camp speaking to the men in groups, encouraging them and praising them, then he ordered them to water their wine generously, as they would be marching early the next day.

In the command tent, Spartacus and the remaining Gaul, Crixus, praised their fallen comrade, Oenomaus, and got down to the serious business of what was to come. Crixus was all in favour of taking their new-found army and fighting a full war against the Romans, getting more of the Latin tribes to join up and perhaps even, once and for all, destroying Rome and everything it stood for. Spartacus still hoped to get as far away from the Romani as possible. The other more senior centurions, along with Gwenn and Epona, were witness to a heated yet reasoned debate. Epona found herself siding very much with Crixus, while Gwenn agreed with Spartacus.

Either way, winter was approaching and there was little prospect of significant travel, or of any further military engagements. For this reason it was agreed to find an area to spend the winter before making any firm decisions. The army headed south towards the area around and between the towns of Thurii and Tarentum. Here they continued to raid unopposed. Indeed, as before, word of their victories simply swelled their ranks and, while some farmers fought to defend their properties, many more joined and brought supplies with them. Teague and Abbon tagged along with the slave army since winter had now set in and no ships would be willing to take them to Aegyptus before the spring.

They celebrated the Gallic new year festival of Samhain, the Roman midwinter festival of Saturnalia and the Gallic feast of Imbolc, while some of the slaves in this disparate army recognised still other festivals and traditions from other cultures which had been subsumed by the republic. It was a strange time, during which the celebration of their first few victories was slowly replaced by anticipation and hope for more in the coming year. Most of the slaves yearned to be as far away from Roman lands as possible, dreaming of being able to return to their homeland or to any safe place; each Campanian or Samnite who felt they had not got what they deserved after the last social war yearned to hurt Rome in any way possible.

There was more than enough time for Epona and Gwenn to irritate each other as they usually did when there were no distractions. They didn't go on raiding sorties so there were few enough injuries and these not too serious. There was a bout of sickness which raced through the slave army in less than a week and then lasted another week before it had passed, leaving everyone a little drained, but all would be fighting fit by spring. Had the Romans known about this sickness, they would perhaps have risked attacking Spartacus even in winter, but they had no intelligence reports on the slave army other than its position and that it was able to raid and settle in and around towns with impunity. There were no problems at all with supplies except for Gwenn and Epona's stocks of medicinal herbs and plants which they could not easily replace at least until spring, and then not everything grew in the region. They would have to make do with what they could find and hope that there were few serious engagements early on.

As spring emerged early in the far south of the peninsular, and the sun soothed the waters of the Sinus Tarentinus and the Ionian Sea beyond, the slave army arranged chariot races to honour Mars and thank the god of war for their victories of the previous year. They also paid homage to Liber and Libera. Any boys in the entourage who were close to sixteen years of age were brought forward and officially declared men, although they had all been armed and equipped for battle some time before. None had a bulla to give up in the ritual, so each was given some token for that purpose. No-one in the slave army was going to pass up the chance to honour the Gods of freedom.

Eventually, Teague and Abbon parted ways with their mother and Gwenn. As the slave army was preparing to move and commence campaigning, the two young men headed towards Tarentum to find a ship. They had learned that the main Roman port was Brundisium on the Mare Adriaticum, but as ever, they felt more at home away from the centre of Roman life if that were possible and Tarentum, while no longer a major port, had its roots in the Hellenic people who founded the town and built it into one of the largest cities in the known world long before Rome even existed. The Romans, for their part, built the Via Appia to Brundisium instead of Tarentum, diverting almost all shipping to Brundisium.

Nevertheless, there were still ships which plied routes in and out of Tarentum and across the Sinus Tarentinus. Although the ships were usually smaller and made more local journeys, to Sicilia or Nicopolis for example, there would be the occasional trading vessel making the crossing of the Mare Magnum to Alexandria or, if no such ship was likely, they would have to make the journey in stages, sailing to Nicopolis and finding another ship there.

32

The slave army was preparing to move out of their winter camp, planning to head north from Thurii. It was a huge force, consisting now of some seventy thousand armed men and a small supporting group of women and other non-combatants. Nevertheless, despite the effective leadership of Spartacus, it was not a cohesive fighting force, nor was everyone loyal to a single general. Many preferred to follow the Gaul Crixus, who disagreed with Spartacus about their objectives. The two argued forcefully before the army decamped.

News came that Rome had finally taken the threat of the slave army seriously and they had dispatched full legions under the direct command of that year's consuls, Lucius Gellius Publicola and Gnaeus Cornelius Lentulus Clodianus.

Crixus was bursting with martial confidence.

"I say we should march on Rome. Take them head on. You've seen how their forces crumble before us. Luck is with us. Lugh is watching over us. Bellenos and Toutatis fight by our side."

Spartacus was grim faced but filled with a kind of savage amusement.

"They have finally decided to take us seriously. Soon we will face our greatest test yet. Yes, Crixus, they have fallen easily to our swords because, my friend, they were just militia. Even the praetorian legions were not the best that Rome has to offer. Yes, we can beat them - with good fortune, we can smash them - but I have no wish to march on Rome itself. Do you imagine they will not raise every single man who can bear arms to stand in our way? Of course they will."

"But with every victory we grow stronger. With every victory we gain more weapons and armour, we are joined by more and more men who hate and despise Rome just as much as we do. They have become the architects of their own destruction with their arrogance and brutality."

"Grand words, and grand talk Crixus. Did not your tribe fall before them?"

"And did not yours also," Crixus spat back.

Spartacus was the first to break the silence.

"We should not be fighting each other. The consular armies lie somewhere to the north of here, and whether we seek to escape, or to crown ourselves dictator, we must either fight them or slip past. I seek to do the latter, but if you wish to throw yourself at them be my guest. Our forces are too large anyway. We should divide and separate. You may create a welcome distraction as I head towards Cisalpine Gaul."

"Agreed. I believe many of those from the Italian tribes will join me. They have no love for Rome. There are some good fighters among the Marsi and Samnites."

"Not only the experienced fighters but also many of the farmers too," Spartacus agreed.

"And should I gain early victories, no doubt more will flock to our cause. I should like to march one hundred thousand men right through the Colline gate."

Gwenn had become a close associate of the Thracian leader, although nobody knew anything about her beyond that she had some sort of mystical power. Rumours spread about her, and Gwenn felt no desire to correct them or give more information to anyone. She was content to be a rumour, a mysterious wise woman, advising Spartacus and bringing him good fortune. She didn't even take offence when the rumour added that she was his lover. It made no difference to her either way since nobody really knew who she was.

Epona, however, remained loyal to Crixus. Besides, her aims were much closer to his anyway. After the leaders had made their plans, it was the turn of Gwenn and Epona to argue through their choices for the future.

"Will you be coming with us to Cisalpine Gaul, or will you join Crixus and attempt to march on Rome?" Gwenn asked her friend.

"You know I will march on Rome, and see it burn to the ground if I can."

"When did you become so bloodthirsty, Epona?" Gwenn looked genuinely sad.

"I believe it is us or them. You know the stories. You know how they have grown more powerful with every passing generation. The story of Brennus has been told as a tale of heroism and Gallic courage, but it should have been told as a warning. The Romani are bitter as mistletoe and as rotten to the core as a dead oak. And just like the mistletoe they are poison; just like the oak they will come crashing down eventually."

"And what will replace them? King Crixus and Queen Epona, and an army of former slaves and angry Italian farmers?"

"Anything is better than the arrogant Romans with their supercilious sneers."

"You really hate the Romani don't you?"

"Not all of them. I haven't spent all this time with you helping the sick of Rome and Campania without seeing that ordinary people are generally good. I have the utmost sympathy for these poor slaves who have been treated worse than animals. But the patricians in their togas, looking down their massive noses at you with undisguised disgust? I long to see their stupid heads on a spike outside the city gates to warn all people not to be arrogant."

Gwenn was genuinely shocked. "What of your oath to do no harm, to protect your people - and all people - to the best of your ability"

"People. I don't know if the Romani patrician can be counted as such. They act like they are Gods. Besides, they seem to be slowly destroying my people and the only way to stop them is to destroy them first. I am old and have one chance left to save my people from the scourge of the Romani. I won't let it be said that I did not do all I could."

"Is this about that stupid prophesy?"

"The prophesy that the Romani will conquer all of Gaul and that my son, Blyth, is the only one who can stop them? You think that is stupid?"

"How Lugh's name do you manage to interpret the prophesy in that way?"

"It is perfectly clear."

"It is nothing of the sort; no prophesy is ever clear. Do you know the story the Helleni tell; of Croesos of Lydia who sought to know if he would win a war against Kuros of the Achaemenid empire? The Oracle at Delphi said that if he went to war, an empire would fall. He assumed that meant the empire of his enemies. Well, he went to war and, sure enough, an empire did fall: his."

"Kaito believes that Blyth must stop the Romani, and The Deru-Weido-Maywr is no fool such as Croesos."

Gwenn gave up. She lifted her cup of wine, unwatered as they both preferred it, and said, "I will miss you Epona, but may Lugh watch over you.

33

The fire crackled and spat as the fat dripped off a rabbit carcass that was suspended above it on a greenstick. Epona poured wine into her cup and passed the jar along to the next man, a wiry Samnite farmer with a growing fuzz of dark stubble on his tanned face. She passed the water jug on without using it. The Samnite liberally watered his wine and then in turn passed to a tall muscular slave whose shaved head was growing out pale blonde. Epona had discovered he was of the Cimbri, like Gwenn, taken as a slave when just a child. The next man along was of Hellenic origins, olive skinned with flowing black hair, as many from the coastal towns along the south of the peninsular were, and, despite generations of being dominated by Rome, owed more culturally to Sparta than to Rome. He answered to the name Iounios. The last was darker than the others, his face glowing a rich amber in the firelight, his eyes seeming larger than life as the whites stood out against his skin, and his smile glinting as he laughed at a joke. Epona had seen Africans before, of course, but had not spent much time with any until these last few weeks. He was called Africanus; Epona had attempted to find out his original name but had then been unable to pronounce it. She liked him. He had suffered appalling treatment as an agricultural labourer, but he was always cheerful and optimistic. He bore no ill will against any but his masters. His reason for joining and fighting was idealistic. He did not seek to kill Romans for the sake of revenge, but simply to free other slaves.

The rabbit looked ready. Epona deftly hooked the stick up and held the ends gently; they were still hot. With the seared and bubbling meat on an earthenware plate she cut the legs off and apportioned the meat as fairly as she could to each man.

The Samnite wiped his mouth.

"Are you not having any?"

Epona looked serious as she replied, "I can't eat. Publicola's legions are a spear's throw away, and he will surely attack tomorrow if we don't first."

"Well I for one can't wait. It's been too long since this sword tasted Roman blood. By next winter, we could be marching into Rome in a triumph, patrician captives in caged carts behind us."

"I admire your optimism," Epona said.

The Samnite visibly slumped. "You're right of course. It may take years. My people have been fighting them since before they were even a great power. Somehow, they always came back from every defeat with another legion, and another."

Nobody else spoke, so the Samnite took this as an invitation to continue telling the story of his tribe's wars against the Romans.

"The history of my people is at least as old as that of Rome. Indeed, when the city of Rome was first founded, our ancestors were already a powerful tribe, even holding power over the young city. We fought alongside them against raiders from the north, but then later, as they grew stronger, the Romans began to interfere with our affairs and we were forced to take up arms against them. Yet there is a story which is told of how the Samnites completely defeated the Romans without ever drawing a sword."

"You killed them with spears?" the Cimbrian guessed.

"Neither swords nor spears," the Samnite declared with a twinkle in his eye, glancing around the fireside.

"Slingers?" Epona suggested.

"Not slingers, nor archers either."

The African scratched his chin and then said, "Did they trap them in a gorge then rain down rocks upon their heads?"

"Half right!" the Samnite laughed. "We trapped them in a gorge, yes. They had no water to drink, and there were only two ways out; both we had blocked and there was no possible escape."

"So you waited until they all died of thirst?" Epona asked in awe.

"Not even that."

"So how did you kill them?" Africanus demanded.

"I never said we killed them," the Samnite grinned impishly.

"What? Yes you did!" roared the Cimbrian.

"I actually said we defeated them."

Epona had to admit that he had.

"So go on, explain what happened then."

This was a story told to young Samnites at their mother's knee. He could tell it in his sleep.

"Our armies were led by Gaius Pontius who was a meddix, the equivalent of a consul. He had succeeded in trapping the Roman army in the gorge known as the Caudine Forks where they had no access to fresh water, but he did not know what to do next; he was young and inexperienced. He sent a messenger to his father, Herrenius Pontius, to ask for advice. The advice came back to make an alliance with Rome in exchange for letting the entire army go free unharmed. The younger Pontius did not like the advice, so he sent another messenger who soon returned with the message to kill every single Roman soldier, and anyone else with them.

"Now he was even more confused. He wondered if one of the messengers had completely misunderstood his father, or if his father had changed his mind in between the two messengers. Either way, he needed to know what to do, and soon, because the Roman soldiers would surely run out of their own water supplies and would die of thirst anyway. He did not want to be known as the general who won battles by depriving the opposing armies of water, like a cruel and inhuman coward. He sent a third messenger asking his father to explain his conflicting advice. When the messenger returned it was with Herrenius himself. Pontius begged him to suggest a middle way, between killing all the Romans, or letting them go free and unharmed. Herrenius was unmoved and insisted that only one of the two extremes would do. Either they must destroy the entire Roman army and leave them helpless to retaliate, or they should show such extreme kindness and generosity in victory that the Romans would be forever grateful to them and agree to a mutual peace. Sadly Pontius could take neither course, and instead, although he agreed to terms of peace with the Romans, and he allowed their armies to go free, he forced them all to walk under the yolk."

There was a collective gasp. All around the campfire knew this was a terrible humiliation. For a Roman soldier to be forced to walk under a line of their own spears held by their captors was the greatest dishonour they could be made to endure.

"Of course, instead of making the Romans into allies and friends, or destroying their army so that they could never oppose us again, we gave them back their army and made of them implacable enemies who would never forgive the insult they had endured. Yes, we won further victories, but you don't need me to tell you that although we won many battles, the Romans eventually won the war. Had it been otherwise, we would not be sitting here awaiting a battle with Publicola's legions in the morning."

34

The fire flickered on and it was Epona's turn. She told, of course, the story of Brennus, the terrible defeat he inflicted on the Romans at the River Allia and the subsequent sack of Rome. She recounted how Brennus had been weighed against the gold he had forced the Romans to pay and had shouted 'Vae Victis' when they complained, but that they had left the young city alone to fester their hatred for the Gauls. Just like the Samnites, they had insulted Rome but not destroyed it, a mistake Epona had no intention of making if she ever had the chance to decide. The wine was passed but, conscious of the coming battle, nobody partook too heavily. The fire flickered and faces turned to Africanus who, it seemed, had stories of his own.

"As a child I was told stories of a great general who took on the Romans and defeated them against overwhelming odds."

All eyes turned to him, awaiting more of the story.

"My people were from Africa, of course, and many generations ago we were sworn enemies of the Romans. We fought so many battles against them over hundreds of years. Our most famous general of all was Hanniba'al Barq."

"I have heard of him," the Samnite interrupted. "We were allies with your people in those wars."

"Yes, that is as I recall it as well. Now at that time, although we had been trading across all the central sea and beyond, we had lost control of the seas to the Romans. Hanniba'al wanted to bring an army to Rome, but it was not possible to travel by sea and, as you know, there is no direct land route either. So do you know what Hanniba'al did?"

"*I* do, but this is your story," the Samnite grinned in anticipation, watching the reactions of the others around the fire.

Africanus drew in the dirt as he spoke, "He took his entire army, from Carthago all the way west through Numidia, past the pillars of Hercules, into Hispania. There he conquered the tribes of Hispania, and then continued on into Gaul, either defeating the tribes there or making deals with them. Then he continued on, right over the mountains and into Italia."

There were gasps at this and the Samnite chuckled waiting eagerly for the next part.

"Not only did he bring his entire army of twenty legions along with cavalry, pack animals, and all his supplies all that way, but he brought something most Romans had never even seen. He brought elephants!"

He looked around at three blank faces and one Samnite whose grin was fading with disappointment. The effect of this revelation was lost on the Cimbrian and Epona, while the other man, Iounios, knew the word but was unfamiliar with the nature of its meaning.

The Samnite tried to explain, "The other word for them is 'lucabos'," he explained.

"I know the term. The Lucanian cow, but I also know it is not a cow," Iounios admitted. "I don't know what it is, and I can't imagine it. I only know it is like a very large horse with, I have heard, an *arm* on its *head*; which is crazy of course."

"That's it, that's it exactly," Africanus enthused.

They all looked at him, awaiting further information.

"So, how large a horse exactly?" Epona asked.

"Well, of course, I have never seen one myself, but I am told that a man may stand underneath the belly of the elephant and not touch the underside."

"How would the cavalryman mount such a horse?" the Cimbrian asked, reasonably.

"I suppose they used a very high mounting platform," the Samnite proposed. "Such a horse would be a formidable opponent in battle."

"But the arm on its head? Tell us about the arm."

"I only know what you know," Africanus admitted. "It has an arm growing from the front of its head and it can lift a man up and throw him to his death."

There was a collective gasp of astonishment.

"When you think about it, it is a cheering thought that Publicola only has four legions of highly trained Roman soldiers, each armed with a scutum and gladius, to face us in the morning," Epona said with a wry smile.

"I'm looking forward to it now you say that," added the Samnite.

"Just a shame we don't each have an elephant to ride upon," added Iounios, and they all laughed.

"I haven't finished telling you of Hanniba'al Barq yet," Africanus complained.

Attention was focused once more on the deep brown eyes of the African.

"Sadly, many of the elephants did not make it across the mountains because they are not used to the cold. And even then, it was not the elephants, but the brilliance of Hanniba'al which dealt the Romans their most crushing defeat of all time at a place - not too far from here in fact - named Cannae. This was, by the way, after he had already defeated them in two major engagements, but on both those occasions the numbers had been either the same, or in Hanniba'al's favour. At Cannae, the great general was outnumbered. He had no more than ten legions including cavalry, while the Romans had nearly twice that number."

"So, how did he manage such a victory against such overwhelming odds?"

"Firstly, he took great care to decide on what ground the battle would take place. The Romans were eager to fight, knowing they had superior numbers, but

Hanniba'al saw which way the wind was blowing. There was a breeze from the east, so he made sure his army was in the east. That way, the wind would blow dust into the enemy's eyes, and as the sun rose it blinded them. But that was a minor point compared with his battle plan. He knew their infantry was stronger, but he had the superior cavalry: Numidians, Hispanics, and Gallics, who were all expert horsemen.

"At the start of the battle he pressed forward in the centre placing some of his cavalry there, but these retreated early, and the Romans pressed forward into the Carthaginian infantry. Hanniba'al himself led from the centre and kept the ranks tight as they fell back, allowing the Roman forces to push forward. At the same time, the cavalry from the centre joined the flanks where the Roman cavalry were already defeated or had fled the field. Now the Roman infantry were pushing further and further against the Carthaginian lines which slowly wrapped around the Romans on three sides. As the Romans realised what was happening it was already too late to respond. The only way out of the trap was back the way they had come, except that now the cavalry came down upon their rear and closed off even that escape."

There was silence, but for the crackling of flames and the hissing of sap from a log.

"Not one legionary walked from the field that day. The consul Lucius Aemelius Paullus was killed, while the other, Gaius Terentius Varro was humiliated. Hanniba'al's army only grew stronger as more Italian tribes joined his cause."

The sap hissed and spat until Epona quietly said, "So, why then do we not see statues to Hanniba'al in the Forum, or Roman affairs overseen from Carthago?"

"Because of course, the Romans never ever give up. Hanniba'al offered them terms but they always refused. It is said that they recruited criminals and slaves into the legions. Whatever happened, even though Hanniba'al won more battles, eventually the tide turned, and the Romans won the war in the end. Hah! We know slaves can fight, right?" he laughed.

It was a bittersweet moment. They knew that this slave army faced a terrible battle in the morning, and they hoped that Crixus would prove himself to be, if not the equal of Hanniba'al, then at least that of Spartacus.

35

"You know, my people too have inflicted a terrible defeat upon the Romans and, in the same way, the Romans came back and destroyed us completely."

Everyone now turned to the Cimbrian, who had spoken slowly and quietly, his voice breaking with emotion.

"I know much of your story already," Epona said softly. "My friend Gwenn who has gone with Spartacus was of the Cimbri tribe as well. Tell us your story?"

"I have never seen the lands my ancestors called home but, when I was a child, I was told the story. Long before I was born there were terrible floods that wiped out whole villages and left farms under the sea. My people were uprooted and roamed the lands for years, carrying all their possessions with them. We were homeless and were not welcome in any of the places we tried to settle. Although our men and women are big and strong, and we can fight when we have to, all we really wanted was to farm in peace. It is no life for a young boy growing up in the back of a cart pulled by mules along bumpy tracks from one place to another while your father fights against one tribe after another.

"We found a place, near a big river, where it seemed there would be some chance that we could settle down, but then it was the Romans who tried to stop us. We had fought our whole lives by then, and even though they sent a huge army, I think maybe ten or twenty legions, my mother told me they were led by fools who were more interested in fighting with each other than against us. When we attacked them, we expected them to put up some sort of a fight, but instead we went through them like a scythe through a field of wheat. Many threw themselves in the river, *some of them in full armour*, and tried to swim away! Even their generals fled like cowards."

Epona added, "And yet, just like Carthago before and Brennus before that, the Romans eventually came back from complete defeat and turned the tide." And then more quietly, more to herself than anyone else, she muttered, "Gwenn was right."

She got up and returned to Crixus' tent. but that night she hardly slept.

In the morning Crixus' armies moved from their position near the town of Sipontum to face the consular legions under the command of Publicola in the shadow of Mount Garganus. As Epona was climbing the slopes to their right, to get a good viewpoint for using her sling, the sun rose behind the allied forces and she was reminded of Haniba'al's strategy. It was to be the only tactical advantage they achieved that day.

While the two opposing forces were evenly matched in numbers, they were not in ability. Without the brilliant tactical mind of Spartacus there, this was the first real test of Crixus' leadership skills and he was found wanting.

Despite scoring some impressive hits from her elevated position, Epona watched all her hopes and dreams being smashed to bloody pieces on the battlefield as row upon row of the relatively inexperienced slave army fell to the ruthlessly efficient thrusting swords of fully trained Roman legionaries. She could just make out the cheerful and positive Africanus disappear in a mass of bodies, the Cimbrian impaled by a pilum, Iounios smashed in the face with a scutum then impaled by a gladius, and the Samnite falling in similar fashion. When the defeat became obvious, the remaining tatters of Crixus' force scattered, discarding armour and weapons in their haste to escape. For Crixus, no such dishonour could possibly be an option, and he went down swinging his sword in the thickest part of the battle. Indeed, as a spear impaled him, he hacked off the head of the man who had driven it in.

Epona collected some more stones from the ground and let loose a last few volleys from her sling until there was no ammunition left. She was weeping bitterly, her face smeared with dirt as she wiped the tears from her eyes to get a better aim, but it was futile. She knew more than ever the feeling of utter hopelessness when faced with an enemy who will never back down, who will never give up, never surrender, an enemy that would keep coming back until there was nobody left to fight them.

She climbed higher, looking for some solid ground where she could descend at a safe distance from Publicola's legions. She slipped and scrabbled as rocks came loose, her staff, in this situation, more hindrance than help. Eventually she reached flatter ground and some sort of trackway. Her fingernails were bleeding, her clothes muddy and torn, and her spirit more broken than it had ever been. She needed to get back to Gwenn, to warn her of the terrible fate that awaited them when they came face to face with a real consular army. She didn't even know where to find her friend. 'Somewhere to the north,' she thought.

36

Aegyptus was nothing like either Teague or Abbon had expected, but it was more than either of them could have imagined. They had both seen Rome, with its massive walls, its vast towering insulae, marble columns supporting myriad temples to uncountable Gods, vast open forums, grand villas marching up the Palatine, and heaving bustling crowds but, while it had obvious opulence and was considerably larger than the city where Alexander the Great was buried, it was as nothing next to the sheer exuberant grandeur of this hot gleaming city whose jaw-dropping effect began before you even arrived.

With the city of Alexandria itself still out of sight beyond the horizon, they could see the top of the Pharos lighthouse. The captain had pointed it out to them with proprietorial pride, although he himself certainly had no part in its construction. As the ship eased into the wide and placid harbour it towered above them, a vast square stone tower rising from a rectangular base which seemed to grow organically from the rocky island on which it stood. The first tower rose many times higher than the ship's mast. Above it was a narrower octagonal tower, also of stone, almost as high as the first, then a third section, a slender circular stone column, rose above that. Near the top of this was the flame itself, capped by a conical top of bronze, oxidised green, which seemed to scrape the sky.

The yellow disc of Bellenos, the sun god, glowered fiercely as it turned the waters into a pulsating carpet of diamonds. The buildings on the harbourside ahead of them gleamed in shades of white, sable, and cream, embellished here and there with darker shades, the rooftops terracotta, mottled sparsely with paler shades of lichens which, unbeknown to any observers present, had taken centuries to grow. Everywhere grew trees and shrubs in every shade of iridescent green, with the occasional flash of a scarlet flower.

In some ways, the straight lines and pale coloured buildings, the rows upon rows of columns, the courtyards, temples, and palaces resembled the finer districts of Rome. The columns of Rome were of white marble, or sometimes plaster over lesser stone, with minimal decoration. Here the columns were also of stone, but each was painted in elaborate designs with deep reds and blues, highlighted with gold leaf. Statues were exuberantly painted, as they were in Rome, but here the colours seemed more intense. Later, on closer inspection, it became clear that this was a once fabulously wealthy city now in decay, while Rome was a newcomer to wealth.

The marketplace beckoned, and Teague and Abbon wandered through the rows of animated sellers, calling their wares in a mixture of the local Hellenic dialect and a language that was quite alien to their ears. The city was an assault on the senses; exotic scents – some pleasant, some not so – reached their nostrils and, in the harsh light, colours seemed more vivid. It was hot, despite being early in the year, the noise was intense, and they were jostled on all sides by other shoppers seeking out the best bargains. Thankfully, the brothers quickly acclimatised to this strange new environment, so that they only noticed the most pungent scents when they passed something like a fish stall, or when a wizened old woman thrust some kind of spice towards them, shouting unintelligibly in her own language. The noise became a hubbub that failed to impinge until a particularly distressed donkey brayed disconsolately under a heavy burden.

Teague, being the eldest, was expected to take the lead although it was Abbon who got talking first to a trader selling fabrics, although Abbon was more interested in the creature which accompanied him. Sitting on top of a rolled-up carpet was a small animal. It seemed to be some sort of hairy homunculus, about the size of a newborn human baby, with an inquisitive black face surrounded by a fringe of pale grey fur while the rest of its head and body was a darker grey. Long slender fingers gripped the edge of the rug, hazel eyes looked intelligently at Abbon with an expectant air, and a long grey tail dangled down.

"What's that?" Abbon asked in Hellenic.

After a moment, while the stallholder mentally identified the language being spoken and adjusted the sounds to match his own dialect of Hellenic, he responded.

"That is Khemi."

The accent was strong but the sentence short enough to ensure comprehension.

"He is good. I like him," Abbon said, keeping his sentences short and simple for clarity.

"He is a little Seth! But I like him too," the stallholder roared with laughter.

Abbon didn't get the joke, but what he really wanted to know was where he could find more animals like this Khemi. Teague had come over now and it took quite some time for them to communicate to the stallholder that they were interested in finding similar animals. The process was hampered in two ways; one was that the trader was relentless in his efforts to show them his wares and discuss the merits of a multitude of fine fabrics and rugs, another was that the animal itself seemed intent on stealing a stoppered jug, while the trader did his best to stop him.

Eventually, after finding out that Khemi was the animal's name, and that he had come from a merchant who travelled to the land called Kush in the south, they tried to explain that they were really interested in another animal, like this but larger, and without a tail. This led to a further discussion which got more and more confused and eventually a suggestion that they try at a place called the Musaeon. By this time, the trader had realised that he was never going to make a sale and so he was keen to get rid of these annoying foreigners. His desire to be rid of them only increased when Khemi finally managed to steal the jug and began to drink from it, spilling a considerable amount of wine as he did so. The trader roared in frustration and grabbed at the jug, while Khemi skittered away dropping the jug on the unfortunate man's head. Teague and Abbon, meanwhile, swiftly made their way in the direction of the Musaeon.

37

The Musaeon turned out to be one of the most impressive buildings in the city and also rather more difficult to gain access to than a common marketplace. At least the dialect of Hellenic spoken by the official looking guards at the main entrance was more familiar to them than had been that of the trader, but the fact remained Teague and Abbon, despite their efforts to dress in the local style, stood out as barbarians with their pale skin and hair and their rough-edged accents.

It fell to Teague to take the lead here as Abbon was not known for his patience. Only after Teague had shown considerable calm determination were they even permitted within the building to plead with more senior officialdom to be allowed further. They were made to wait for quite some time in the cool of an antechamber before eventually another official told them that they would not be permitted to enter the Musaeon today but that they should return on the next day at sunrise.

Teague put a hand on Abbon to warn him to stay calm and they left, with Abbon keeping his temper until he exploded outside with pent up rage. Teague let it wash over him and agreed with Abbon to placate him. They spent a hot night in a rather seedy sort of establishment, which had been all they were able to find, and the next day it was Teague alone who went back to the Musaeon to try again.

Abbon meanwhile continued to explore the rest of the city. Just as in Rome, the streets were laid out in a grid pattern, but unlike Rome it was less crowded and cleaner. Just as they had seen on the first day this was an opulent place in gentle decline rather than a thrusting grubby greedy explosion of new growth. Abbon headed towards the eastern part of the city first. Here, he noticed the houses were less opulent, there was less of the ostentatious use of fluted columns and brightly coloured decoration. Certainly there was no gilding or other obvious signs of wealth, but there was an honest cleanliness that made this part of town the most pleasant. Dark robed men walked in small groups, women in their own groups, and nobody appeared to be doing any work. Abbon wondered how they kept the place so clean if nobody worked. He looked around for slaves going about their business, but there seemed to be none, or very few possible candidates.

He came across a building which seemed like some sort of temple. The front was open and, since nobody seemed to object, he went inside. It was different from other temples in some way that Abbon couldn't quite put his finger on. Then it dawned on him that there were no statues and no paintings of the god or goddess to whom the temple was dedicated. Here there was a little more ornamentation than in the rest of this part of the city, but it was nothing like as ornate and gaudy as Roman or

Hellenic temples usually were. This had some of the simplicity, in fact, of the oak groves of Lugh-dun or Ynys-Mona while still being of clean white stone. The whole place was impeccably clean and pure. The only decoration was a lamp stand in the centre of the entrance. A central pillar rose up from a heavy looking base and then split into a series of branches, in the manner of a carefully pollarded tree, three on either side of the central stem, all parallel to each other, and each with a lamp on the end. The central stem was just a little higher than the other six and bore a lamp which was just a little larger and brighter than the rest. Abbon, so obviously a foreigner, was aware of attracting some mild attention and, when he attempted to proceed further into the temple, he found himself very gently guided away. Since he had no very strong desire to get inside, he ambled towards the exit and with a backward glance at the lamps flickering serenely, he stepped back out into the bright, hot day.

He now decided to head to the opposite side of the city, to the west. As he explored it became obvious this was the poorer part of town. The buildings were more dilapidated, the shops more drab, the streets narrower, and the people less vibrant, subdued, carrying a faint hint of resentment. These were the indigenous inhabitants of a city far older than the man whose name it now bore. He exulted in the name of Aléxandros of Macedon and, in his short life, had conquered almost the entire known world, right to the furthest eastern reaches of the Darius' empire. Here in Aegyptus he had become Pharaoh, the god king. The Helleni had imposed their beliefs and culture on a once proud people who had already been subjugated by the Persians. However, Abbon was unaware of any lingering resentment towards strangers until he stopped at a stall offering melons and other fruit. He tried asking the price in Hellenic and was met with a blank face and a stony silence. He tried again, pointing to a melon, and simply asking, "How much?" while also holding some coins out. The stallholder gave a price which even Abbon knew was insultingly high and his interest in buying a melon evaporated.

Continuing on his way, he passed another temple, this one far more typical of those he had seen in Rome. It was exuberant and gaudy with many statues and frescoes painted in bright colours. Beyond the temple however the demeanour of the whole street returned to one of sultry resentment and soon Abbon felt the sense that he was being followed. He turned down an alley which seemed to narrow still further as it progressed. Glancing behind himself he realised that he was indeed the subject of attention from a couple of very shady looking characters. Further on he realised to his horror that the alley came to a dead end. He was trapped, with a blank wall ahead of him and two men, who he felt sure were not interested in a genial conversation, behind him. He glanced about for some means of escape. There was one other turning but even this, Abbon could see, led only to a wooden door.

He glanced back and saw the men quicken their pace, one of them drawing a long blade from a sheath. Abbon, heart beating fast now, darted down the alley out of sight. When the men reached the corner, they found their quarry had vanished.

38

It was evening now, and Teague was already back at the place where they were staying having had no better results in trying to get into the Musaeon than they had enjoyed on the previous day. Abbon bounced in talking excitedly.

"I've solved the problem!"

"What?"

"How to get into the Musaeon; it's been staring us in the face."

"It has?"

"Yes! I can't believe I had to be chased by men with knives to think of it."

"What? Who chased you? Why? Were you hurt?"

"Do I look hurt? Forget about that, it was nothing. Just some locals who took a dislike to me. I shook them off, but it was only when there was nowhere left to go that I realised how to get into the Musaeon."

"Right. Look, slow down, and more importantly, can you please get to the point?"

"We've been going about it all wrong. We don't need to sit in waiting rooms and talk to officials to get inside, we just climb over the roof and get in that way."

"But then as soon as someone sees us, they will just throw us out again!" Teague sighed, exasperated. He had hoped Abbon had a proper solution.

"But that's just it!" Abbon declared, "They won't. Because we will already be inside."

Teague looked confused, "I don't understand, how will that help?"

"It's obvious. If getting in is so difficult, then anybody who is inside must have been allowed in. Anybody inside will know that, so nobody will question us being in there, once we're in!"

And with that, Teague's face transformed into a mix of respectful wonder at Abbon's brilliance, and stunned annoyance at his own lack of intelligence.

The next morning they set off for the Musaeon and, in a suitably quiet spot, transformed into their cat and squirrel forms. Abbon swarmed straight up the walls as though the smooth masonry were a ladder which, to his tiny squirrel feet, it may just as well have been. Teague tried several routes and had a few failed attempts before he was on top of the roof next to Abbon looking down into a large central garden area with fountains, surrounded by a covered walkway of columns. Robed men - they were exclusively men - walked along in pairs seemingly debating important topics, or sat round reading scrolls or tablets, or writing.

Men of the Wise Oak

The two animals surveyed the scene, looking for an opportunity to jump down and transform without being seen. The plan depended on them looking as though they belonged here. Abbon skittered around the rooftop until he could see there was a balcony at the end below where they had started. From there he could see a staircase going down and some sort of corridor going back from there and branching off. It was unoccupied and offered their best chance. After a few moments' inspection for a suitable route he scampered back and then down a pillar, making use of a convenient climbing plant, and landed on the balcony. Teague followed, rather more awkwardly but nevertheless safely. They glanced around and, since there was nobody here, they transformed back into human form. Taking a moment to adjust and regain some composure they calmly and slowly walked down the staircase chatting about nothing in particular.

A grey haired, bearded man was walking towards them, carrying some sort of intricate device whose purpose they did not recognise. Both Teague and Abbon felt their heartbeats quicken, their conversation dried up as panic began to overcome them. The grey-haired man drew closer, as they looked around the room beyond him, they realised that nearly every head was either bald, or covered in silvery grey hair. They were the youngest men here by far. Abbon regretted his plan and hoped they would simply be thrown out, and not taken for some kind of punishment. The man now drew almost alongside them.

He looked at them with dark amber eyes and said, "I'm looking for Posidonius; have you seen him?"

Teague and Abbon both stalled momentarily. Finally Teague found his voice first.

"Uh, no. No, I'm sorry…"

During this brief exchange, Teague and Abbon were able to see the mechanism up close, although this gave neither of them any clue as to its purpose. It appeared to be some sort of open box, made from wood overlaid with sheets of bronze. Inside and outside where a series of wheels. Each wheel had a row of teeth which interlocked with the teeth on the next wheel along. There were a number of small arms each tipped with a small coloured bead. As Abbon watched, he could see the wheels turning, some quickly, some imperceptibly slowly, and the little beads moved as well, on the ends of the rods holding them. It really was the most extraordinary curiosity.

"Oh, no matter, there he is!" And, with that, the man hurried away carrying the strange-looking mechanism towards a younger man, judging by his relatively dark hair. Presumably this was the aforementioned Posidonius, although neither Teague nor Abbon had heard of him.

39

It seemed as though Abbon's plan had worked after all. Instead of being unceremoniously hauled out and thrown into the street or given some unspeakable punishment for the crime of invading the inner sanctum of learning they had, as Abbon predicted, been presumed to belong simply because they were inside. Teague knew logically that it would work, but he had not managed to convey that confidence to his heart. He could feel himself calming down, the sweat on his palms felt cold now and he wiped them on the cloth of his chiton. They were ambling along with an air of belonging made stronger by their recent success.

Abbon echoed Teague's thoughts, "I thought we were about to be thrown out then, or worse."

"Me too. We should have known better. You did well to think of this. Oh, look."

Teague moved with more purpose now towards a table on which was a roughly square board of some sort of stone, set with a series of circular discs of ivory. The stone was inlaid with a series of criss-crossing lines of a different coloured stone meticulously inlaid into it by a master craftsman. The circular discs bore strange markings, in red on one set, and black on the other. The markings didn't quite look like pictures, but they were too complex to be any form of writing that Teague knew.

"Is this a version of that game you play?" Abbon asked.

"No. Well... maybe? I don't think so though. I don't know."

"Well, I'm glad we got that sorted then."

Teague continued to ponder over the pieces while Abbon watched and waited for a more enlightening answer from Teague.

A soft voice came from behind them and made them start once more. "I see you are interested in Shang-Chi then?"

Teague and Abbon turned around and both looked blankly at the wiry old man who strongly resembled Kaito.

"The game," he went on, "it is called Shang-Chi, which I understand to mean elephant game, but the meaning is not so important."

"I don't think we have ever seen this game before," Teague said.

"Of course you haven't," the man laughed, and the corners of his eyes twinkled and creased up just like Kaito's would when he laughed.

"We've seen a game that looks a bit like it, but not the same," Abbon added, not wanting them to look like fools.

"Would you like me to teach you the rules?"

"Well, if it is not too much trouble?" Teague began.

"No trouble at all! The truth is, I can't get a decent game, even here. So many wise men, so few with any time for games. But, I say to them, a game of strategy can teach you much about the world and its problems. But they turn to their scrolls and roll their eyes and sigh," he chuckled.

Teague and Abbon smiled to humour him.

The game did indeed have similarities to that which Kaito had taught them so many years ago, but there were enough differences that Teague lost the first game fairly soundly. He won the next, and the third. Abbon held his own for a reasonable while until the old man got a victory which restored some of his injured pride at being beaten by a beginner.

Some hours had passed, and they had not really learned anything about where to find the creatures they were looking for, but they had made a friend of sorts who had access to the inner sanctum.

They had discussed the similarities and differences between Shang-Chi and the war game that Kaito had taught them, while they were playing. Teague had then suggested that he bring his game set in tomorrow and the old man was clearly interested. They left via the main entrance attracting one or two surprised glances from the bureaucracy who had spent so much time preventing them from entering before now. The old man gave his own personal assurances that these two young men were to be admitted without delay in the morning and the two brothers departed with wide smiles and headed for the nearest inn for a celebratory drink.

The next morning at first light, they took Teague's board and pieces with them to the Musaeon where, despite their concern that, somehow, they might still be refused entry, they were ushered through without any delay whatsoever. Inside, they quickly found the old man who looked so much like their own great grandfather and revealed the set to him. His eyes lit up as though he had planted wheat and harvested gold.

"This is most interesting. It looks similar as you say, but not exactly the same. The diagonal lines are the most obvious difference before you even set it up."

Teague arranged the pieces in their correct positions and began to explain the main differences in how they moved. Eventually, the old man said he was ready for a game and they played. Although he looked like he might be winning at one point, he eventually fell to Teague's superior tactics.

"You have a remarkable talent for this sort of game, young man."

Abbon cut in, "He beats everyone. Only Kaito can defeat him, and even then, only sometimes."

"Kaito? Not Cato the censor, you're both too young to have met him. But surely… are you referring to Kaito Drusophos?"

Teague's mind was quicker than Abbon's as they both made the connection.

"Yes, Drusophos, the Deru-Weido. He is the father of our grandfather."

"And you knew him while he was alive?"

"He is still alive," Abbon said with a note of surprise.

"Is he?" the man looked genuinely astonished.

"He was, the last time we saw him, but that was quite some time ago," Teague told him honestly. "He was going in search of our older brother who was in some sort of trouble."

"But he must surely be more than one hundred years old now? Did he visit the lands of the Macrobioi and partake of the fountains of youth?"

"I don't… know…" Teague had to admit, since he had no idea what the old man was talking about.

"Well, no matter. Any descendant of Kaito Drusophos…" he hesitated, thought for a moment, and then went on, "Oh, but that also means you are also the sons of Trethiwr."

"Yes," the two boys chorused.

"And now the next generation of Drusophos comes to Alexandria and I have lived to meet them. You have a great deal to live up to."

40

News had come to Spartacus of the defeat of Crixus' army a few days afterwards when runners caught up with him, bearing the bad news. Some of those who had escaped the slaughter at Garganus also eventually found their way to rejoin the main army of Spartacus, which had been moving steadily northwards through the hills, avoiding the roads and the city of Rome itself. Among them was Epona who had regained some of her composure but none of her confidence.

"They won't stop. They'll never stop until every last one of us is dead. It's hopeless. We can't win, we can't break even, and we can't stop fighting. I watched them, the legions. I watched them from the hillside looking down, they just stand firm, tight together, thrust and move, thrust and move, always forwards. They stab with their swords, and smash with their shields. Stab and smash, stab and smash, until there's nobody left to stab or smash anymore and they have won. And just like the others said, around the campfire, even if you win a battle, even if you completely destroy a legion, there will be another, and another, and another, until you have nothing left to fight with," Epona sobbed.

Gwenn placed a cup of wine in front of her. "Which others?"

Epona, between heaving sobs, told her all about Crixus, and how he had fought right up until the end. She told about her friends; the Samnite, the Cimbrian, Iounios, and Africanus. How each had recounted stories of terrible defeats meted out to the Romans, and how each time the Romans had come back from defeat to win victory. She took gulps of wine, like a small child who has only recently learned to drink, and told of how she had then watched each and every one of them slain in the ensuing battle.

"I'm sorry," Gwenn said.

"You were right," Epona whispered hoarsely.

"That's not important," Gwenn said.

"It is. We can't fight them. We have to get away. As far away as possible."

"We must fight them. The word from our scouts is that Publicola's victorious legions are pursuing us from the south, and somewhere to the north Clodianus is making plans to intercept us. If we are to escape, we must surely go through one or the other."

Epona let her head slump onto the table in front of her.

"Drink your wine and call to Bellenos for aid," she groaned.

They were indeed forced into battle. Some two weeks after the defeat of Crixus they came face to face with the untested legions of Clodianus. They were a few days march north of Rome in a narrow valley. Epona took up a position on a hillside and prepared for the inevitable destruction of her friends. Gwenn was with the main body although not in the front lines. Despite her size and her proven fighting ability she was still merely a woman. Besides, Spartacus reasoned, she was far more useful in giving aid to the injured than in the thick of the battle. Gwenn didn't mind as she really had no stomach for the relentless bloodshed of a pitched infantry battle. Epona was pleased because she had seen too many good friends crushed under Roman calligae. However, Spartacus yet again proved himself the better general as he led his army in a glorious victory against Clodianus. The reputation of Spartacus was such that many legionaries fled the field before they had even engaged in battle. Many more were captured or killed because of this, but Spartacus wasted no time before rounding on the advancing legions of Publicola. He headed south, seeking to engage them in battle before they were ready and before they could learn of the defeat of Clodianus. Filled with confidence, they used the road and, just three days later, Spartacus defeated Publicola in similar fashion to the previous victory.

Once again, Spartacus set about collecting weapons and armour and organising funeral pyres for the dead. There were a large number of captives, which was a new problem for him to deal with since there were no means by which they could be held. Some begged to join the slave army. Spartacus knew they could never be trusted, and so refused. Instead, he organised funeral games, in honour of his friend Crixus and the other men who had been killed at Garganus. Three hundred legionaries were kitted out as Gauls or Thracians and forced to fight to the death until none were left standing. Gwenn and Epona watched in silence, seeing the slave army cheering and screaming for blood, for vengeance, becoming more like the people they were fighting as every day passed. Neither woman spoke but both knew at least some of what the other was thinking.

With the games over and the pyres burning down to embers the slave army now moved towards Picenum and the Mare Adriaticum. Despite the single defeat at Garganus the army had grown continually. Spartacus now commanded some ninety thousand men, with many thousands of women and children in the party as well, and even now some babies born since the campaign had started; such is the nature of human beings even in war. The shattered and demoralised consular legions returned to Rome to re-equip and regroup, then they gave chase once more. They engaged Spartacus once again in the north of Picenum and once again their troops deserted the field rather than face the onslaught of this seemingly invincible gladiator-turned-general. Only the legions of Cisalpine Gaul remained in his path, numbering some ten thousand men and led by Gaius Cassius Longinus Varus. Spartacus defeated these with some ease and Varus barely escaped with his life.

It was now autumn, harvest time, and rather than attempt an alpine crossing now, with winter on the way and few provisions, Spartacus instead decided to take advantage of the fertile plains and allowed his men to rest, giving them free reign to loot and pillage whatever they needed for food and anything else.

As confidence grew among the well-fed forces of Spartacus' army the talk turned away from escape and back towards taking the fight to Rome. Many were the conversations in which those whose home had always been in Italia persuaded those who longed to return to Gaul, Thrace, Numidia, Pontus, Cillicia and other homelands which they could scarcely remember, to turn instead and attack Rome, or at least Roman interests in Italia.

"We defeated their militia, we defeated their praetorian legions, and we have even defeated their consular legions. Who can stop us now? Nobody. Spartacus is the greatest general since Marius."

There were appeals to vengeance.

"What about the funeral games, when we forced those Romans to fight to the death! Do you really think we have taken enough from these people who took your freedom and made you less than human?"

Appeals to bravery worked as well.

"You aren't going to run away now, are you? Think of the honours that you will earn, the respect of your fellow fighters. I hear we captured silver; there may be phalerae to be won for those who show the greatest courage."

The tide of opinion turned inexorably as even Spartacus felt emboldened by their successes. They were well fed and well equipped. Their numbers had swollen to nearly one hundred thousand fighting men as well as thousands of followers. As the first cold of winter blew down from the Alps the decision was made to head for the south once more. Spartacus had convinced himself, or allowed himself to be convinced, that they should adopt a new plan. He would get his army to Sicilia where he would easily overcome the governor and then recruit the vast number of slaves who worked on the huge latifundia producing grain to feed Rome. They would rule over Sicilia and use it as a base. From there they might perhaps be able to launch attacks on Rome, or even simply trade with Rome who would pay any price to get grain for fear of their own citizens rising up in revolt. There were still those, particularly among the Gallic and Germanic stock who were determined to escape from Italia altogether. Many who had young children took their leave and aimed for the lower passes. Gwenn and Epona discussed their options and, in the end, decided to stay with Spartacus. His reputation held a huge fascination for them, just as it did for Roman citizens in the city, terrified that this slave army would turn finally on them and wondering where the general was who could save them from this terrifying menace.

41

In Rome, meanwhile, there had been uproar and fear in equal measure. Word of the brilliance of Spartacus had spread. He had defeated every army sent against him and it seemed there was nobody with the skill, courage, or good fortune who would be able to defeat him. It was surely only a matter of time before he marched his slave army on the city itself, and then what? Would the walls hold him? And if so, for how long? Publicola and Clodianus had not acquitted themselves well and, on their return from their most recent failure in Picenum, they were politely but unequivocally relieved of their commands. There was only one man who seemed both willing and able to take command of an army that might have any chance of success against Spartacus. His name was Marcus Licinius Crassus.

Crassus was extremely wealthy, having bought up property seized from supporters of Marius during Sulla's proscriptions. While everyone else appeared frozen in fear of the slave army, Crassus was itching to be given command of fresh legions. The senate now took the threat more seriously than ever and Crassus was given command of eight legions, six which he would recruit himself, and a further two being the remnants of the four which had been commanded by Publicola and Clodianus.

It was late evening in the legionary camp in Picenum, where the two remaining consular legions of that year were awaiting new orders. Word had arrived that both consuls had been relieved of command and that six fresh legions under Marcus Licinius Crassus were on their way to take over in what was now openly referred to as a war, no longer were they treating it as a minor incident or an uprising.

"Thank the Gods," muttered Sextus, a young and inexperienced legionary, when the decanus had passed on the news.

He was carefully carving small slivers of wood from a piece of tree root. He had been working on it for a long time. For days it had seemed to be just a lump of brownish wood. Now, it was finally taking shape. It was a beautiful and very lifelike miniature owl, the grain of the wood suggesting feathers. Two hard knots of darker wood had been artfully contrived to form the eyes.

"Don't imagine that there will be no consequences when Crassus gets here," the decanus warned.

He was a seasoned campaigner who had seen his fair share of fighting, but even he had fled from their last battle with the Spartacani. Better to flee and live to fight another day, he reasoned, but he had seen others who looked like they had no wish to fight on any day.

"Crassus can hardly complain when we were outnumbered, and their general seems to have the Gods at his back," complained another legionary, named Gnaeus. "What would he expect us to do?"

"I have not served under Crassus myself, but if I know anything of his reputation, he would expect you to stand still and kill as many of the enemy as you could before you died. More importantly, he would expect us to stand shoulder to shoulder, scutum to scutum, and never flee the field unless under the direct orders of the centurion."

The eight legionaries and their two auxiliary servants were a mixed bunch, with some being old buddies and others newly added. This was inevitable under the circumstances. The original four legions had been defeated so many times, and lost so many men, that they were now just two legions. There had been regroupings of every division, from cohorts right down to contubernia, the ten men who shared a tent.

"Perhaps with someone like Crassus leading us, and fresh legions to increase our numbers, then we stand a chance," Sextus reasoned.

He was the youngest and newest member of the tent. He held up the little owl to assess his work before setting about removing some more small slivers.

"If you don't mind me asking," began another legionary who went by the name Rufus, "why did you join the army anyway? You don't seem the type."

Sextus looked a little aggrieved but then admitted, "I didn't really have much choice. My family are not wealthy. We had a little land once, a long time ago, but you know how it is now. All the land is owned by a few wealthy men and worked by slaves. I'm good with my hands, but you can't just decide to be a carpenter, you have to be trained. Since the days of Marius, everyone like me who can't find work and has no land has at least got the opportunity to join the legions and, if we survive, perhaps to make our fortune."

There was a commotion at the far northern end of the camp. Suddenly they were being roused for battle. At night! The decanus was shouting orders and hurriedly getting into his armour. The men began to form up into ranks and prepare for whatever was to come when the rumour spread that it was Spartacus and his army heading back from the north.

"But I thought they were heading for the alps and Gaul?"

"I heard they were headed east to Thrace. That's where Spartacus is supposed to be from, isn't it?"

"No, he was a gladiator who fought as a Thracian, but that doesn't mean anything. He could be from anywhere."

"Maybe he was defeated by the governor of Gallia Cisalpina?"

"Gaius Cassius Longinus? With a single legion? I don't think so."

As the realisation that this was indeed the slave army gradually sank in, fear rippled through the ranks. Such was the terror inspired by Spartacus now, that the lines were already thinning even as they began to form.

Men were disappearing into the night, their armour cast aside to speed their flight. When the clash happened there was almost no resistance at all from the Romans. Those who remained were slaughtered and their weapons and armour seized, as had been the routine in every encounter so far.

42

Crassus arrived to find a rag-tag army of terrified legionaries, mostly wearing nothing but tunics: their armour seized, their dignity in shreds. White with rage, he gave a number of orders to his tribunes who then set about carrying them out.

When the remainder of the four consular legions were assembled there were some twelve cohorts left: around six thousand men, or just over a single legion.

Crassus stood with his six fresh legions behind him and issued his orders that the twelve cohorts must divide into groups of ten and draw lots. As the orders were relayed by the centurions there was a murmur that grew as men began to realise what he had planned. Marcus Licinius Crassus intended to revive an ancient tradition of the Roman army. Grim faced, the decanus held ten straws in his fist as each member of his contubernum chose their fate. Sextus drew a long straw as did Gnaeus, and each in turn drew a long straw until there was only one left in the clenched fist of the decanus. His head drooped slightly, but he made no sound. Sextus sobbed briefly then shouted, "No!"

"Calm down lad," the decanus soothed. Did he really have to be brave, even now, for this raw recruit, he wondered.

"But…"

"Be quiet, Sextus," Gnaeus scolded.

Rufus was less patient, "It's time you learned to act like a Roman. We've brought this upon ourselves through cowardice. If you can't even do this, you are no use to any of us and I for one would gladly turn my club on you after we've killed our unlucky decanus."

Men from the new legions were passing out clubs to those who had been lucky in the lots. Sextus still looked horrified. He realised that, what with being inexperienced and therefore usually at the back, and having fled from the last two battles, he had never actually killed a man. He had never killed an enemy soldier, and now he was going to be forced to kill his decanus. He tried to imagine if he had drawn the short straw would he feel any worse. He turned his club around and tried to hand it to the decanus.

"Let me take the short straw."

The decanus looked him squarely in the eye. "I have half a mind to take that from you and beat you to death right now, you coward," he spat, "but it was I who drew the short straw, and I have run from death too many times myself now to do so again. Now get on with it. You must take the first blow; and try to make sure it is fatal!"

He knelt down and bowed his head to give him a good target. "Get on with it then!" he roared, steeling himself not to shake as he awaited the first blow, eyes closed.

Sextus hesitated but the look of white-hot fury from Rufus was enough to make him stir into action. He raised the club and brought it down as hard as possible on the back of the Decanus' head. It was a good strike and might very well have been fatal, but to be sure, the rest of them rained down blows upon the silent immobile body of their former leader. They all wanted to be sure that he was properly dead and would not suffer unduly. All around them were the sounds of six hundred men being brutally clubbed to death by over five thousand of their comrades.

Sextus was sick.

Rufus was right; he really didn't seem the type.

43

Crassus had taken a huge gamble. Decimation was an ancient tradition that had not been used for more than a generation. To kill the enemy was considered noble, but to kill one's fellow legionaries was dishonourable. Even in the many battles that had been fought between different legions, supporting bitter enemies like Marius and Sulla, there had been a reluctance for Romans to kill other Romans in battle, but to murder your own tent mate at close quarters with heavy clubs was sickening: in Sextus' case, literally so. However, Crassus had got away with it.

The mood among his own six legions, many of whom were veterans of previous campaigns under his command, was one of grim determination. They knew he was a good general, and if he felt the punishment was warranted, then they were willing to accept that. Among the remnants of the decimated legion there were mixed feelings, perhaps almost as many emotions as there were men to feel them. Bitterness, anger, sadness, denial, and guilt in varying blends. Foremost among these emotions however was fear; no longer the fear of Spartacus, but fear of their own general, fear of failure, fear of the odium that would stain their name, even after death, fear of ever having to raise a club against one of their own comrades again. That last fear was almost greater than of being the one clubbed to death and it kept young men like Sextus awake at night.

Crassus took command of his troops sure in the knowledge that they feared him more than they feared Spartacus, and he followed that up by catching a small detachment of the main slave army unawares. Some ten thousand of Spartacus' men were killed in the engagement with very few casualties among the legions. The boost to their confidence was incalculable. Sextus' gladius tasted blood for the first time in his hands and the killing only got easier after the first time. Spartacus however reached Bruttium, in the south of Italia, by winter and took the town of Thurii easily. Now was neither a good time for fighting nor for taking ship to Sicilia, even though the island lay just five miles across the straight from Rhegium in the west. Instead, Spartacus took to raiding the area around them, while Crassus undertook a monumental task that only a Roman general would ever consider.

Crassus had decided to build fortifications consisting of a deep ditch and raised ramparts across the entire neck of land laying between the Mare Nostrum and the Sinus Tarentinus, forty miles long, to contain the vast army until he could formulate a plan to deal with them properly.

Neither Crassus, nor any of his legates, nor the tribunes, had any concept that they were about to move three hundred million talents of earth and rubble in a matter of a few weeks. Such measurements were effectively meaningless, and not helpful. To each contubernium there was a length of ditch to dig, a number of stakes to drive in to reinforce the defences, and six thousand talents of soil and rubble that needed to be dug out and piled up to form the ramparts. The legions were more than just the finest military force in the known world, but also engineers who built and repaired roads or walls and, on this occasion, dug ditches. Whatever the task, they would carry it out methodically and with vigour until the job was done or they were ordered to stop.

Among the military tribunes of that year was a young Roman patrician by the name of Gaius Julius Caesar. Crassus was aware of him and had heard good things of his ability to get the job done, but even he was impressed with how efficiently Caesar undertook his part in the monumental task before them. His section was finished in just over a week, and his men began to assist with building the sections on either side of them. Crassus observed how he managed the delicate balancing act of being both a friend and comrade of his men and, at the same time, a respected commander. At just twenty-eight he had been elected as a military tribune at the head of the polls and was clearly headed for great things; perhaps even consul in his time.

44

Teague and Abbon were keen to renew their efforts to find out about Abbon's strange simian. They asked the old man, who confessed great ignorance in such matters, but he did assure them that he knew who they could ask. He introduced them to another man whose name was Zotikos, and then quickly made his excuses and departed swiftly before Zotikos could begin to engage him in conversation.

Zotikos had an unnerving habit of looking slightly to the side as he spoke, and of closing his eyes on those rare occasions when he listened. He constantly went off the topic and rambled at length about some minute detail of the lives of seemingly unimportant creatures. He showed them boards on which rows upon rows of butterflies were fastened using some sort of gum. Neither Teague nor Abbon had any idea that butterflies varied so greatly in form. They held a fleeting fascination as they flitted about among the flowers on warm summer's days, but since they had no known medicinal or food value, they had not been the focus of much interest beyond that.

"It's fascinating, isn't it?" Zotikos enthused.

Not wishing to appear rude and hoping to keep on the right side of him, Abbon and Teague nodded and agreed enthusiastically.

"Some people, even quite educated men, ask me why I want to collect each different type, but knowledge is important simply for its own sake, don't you agree?"

"Oh, yes."

They attempted to steer the effervescent biologist onto the subject of simians and were making some progress when his attention was once more hooked by something that had escaped their attention. They were in the central garden area where a pond sparkled in the sunshine, surrounded by a low wall of a soft dark stone. He stood up and crept towards the wall, reaching into a sinus of his robe and pulling out a small silk bag, which seemed to be mounted on a short stick. Neither Teague nor Abbon could see what it was that had caught Zotikos' attention, but they were grateful for the break in the cataract of words that tumbled from his mouth. They watched as he flicked the bag down onto a part of the wall over a large crack. Another search in the folds of his robe brought forth a small wooden stick the width of a finger and a little longer. He probed into the crack and then something fell into the bag which he lifted up and twisted to keep whatever it was from escaping.

"If this is what I think it is…"

He wandered away, distracted and muttering, then came back a short while later holding a box in his free hand. Placing the box on the table, he tipped the contents of the little bag out into the box. It turned out to be a small dusty coloured, and deeply uninspiring lizard which remained motionless for a moment before surging up the inside of the box as easily as it walked on the bottom. Zotikos clamped a lid down before it could escape. He looked delighted, but before he could explain why, Abbon took the moment to get in with his question first.

"We really would like to know more about simians; specifically a large kind with black fur, and no tail."

"Yes, of course. How inconsiderate of me. I am quite pleased about this find though, you see it's a..."

"The simian!" Teague interrupted.

Zotikos looked taken aback, but asked, "Black fur?"

"And no tail," Abbon repeated.

"I might know the creature you seek, but it is not natural in these parts."

"If you can tell us where we can find them?" Teague asked, breathing deeply to stay calm.

"I can take you to see one here in Alexandria, but it may be dangerous."

"We can take care of ourselves," Teague insisted.

Abbon added, "Can you take us there now?"

Zotikos looked harried, "Well, I…"

Teague gently laid a hand on Zotikos' shoulder and said, "We seek knowledge. Knowledge is so important, don't you agree?" As he spoke he looked straight at

Zotikos who, for once, returned Teague's gaze. For a moment his eyes glazed over before he seemed to come to a decision.

"Yes, we can easily get there and back before the sun sets. Come, let's hurry though."

45

He led them from the Musaeon and quickly along the main street, which was wide enough for several chariots to ride abreast along its length. They were heading to the west of the city, where Abbon had been the day before. It took a long time as Zotikos stopped frequently when something caught his eye. At one point he was down on his hands and knees watching an ant struggling to drag a piece of fruit that was several times larger than itself. Abbon was getting impatient. Teague reminded Zotikos that he had wanted to get to the temple and back during daylight and, reluctantly, he continued walking. Eventually, they reached the gaudy temple not far from where Abbon had been followed. It sat on a hill, elevated above the rough and slightly squalid city around it, the red and gold decoration glinting and glowing in the sun. Then Zotikos led them up the steps into the temple itself. It was a long climb.

"This is the old part of the city. Even now, after many generations, there are people here who resent being ruled over by what they see as a foreign power. It never amounts to anything, unless you wander alone in the narrow streets and become a target for some of the rougher inhabitants."

Abbon thought about his previous visit here and understood why he had been targeted.

"We're safe enough in a group, and during daylight, especially on the main streets. Aléxandros ho Mégas conquered with military might, while the Ptolemaei sought to conquer with culture, and religion. This is the temple to the god Serapis, who takes on both Hellenic and Egyptian features to bring the people of this land closer to our ways. As you see, from the many people coming and going, it works, up to a point. People will make sacrifice to any god as long as they feel he is on their side. Serapis is on everyone's side, so he has many devotees." He smiled.

Teague and Abbon wondered how Zotikos had spare breath to talk as they climbed the stairs in silence, but talk he did, incessantly. He pointed out statues and frescoes, explained how the work was carried out and when. Pointed to sections which had been added after the original building work and other parts where construction had ceased. And all this interspersed with references to animals, most of which meant nothing to Abbon and Teague beyond occasional recognition that such animals existed. They reached the top of the steps and walked across a wide-open paved space to the main temple itself.

"Come. Come inside."

They stepped into the cool interior of the temple and felt the heat of the day disappear along with much of the sound which, until then, they had not noticed. The interior was large and airy, dominated by a vast statue of the god painted and gilded in colours that were to some extent lifelike, yet too much so. It had a vibrancy that went beyond the drab imperfection of mortal colours.

Zotikos whispered, "He's only made of wood."

Neither Teague nor Abbon felt that this fact detracted from the magnificence of the statue, as Serapis towered over them, his features distinctly Hellenic, his trappings more Egyptian.

Worshippers were arriving and leaving offerings with the attending priests. Zotikos recognised one and caught his attention, bowing as he went over to speak to him. Teague and Abbon followed, in the absence of any instructions either way. They listened to a conversation that took place in a language that was alien to them, with just the occasional word in Hellenic that they recognised.

Then the priest turned and walked away with Zotikos following. He indicated with the merest signal that Teague and Abbon should follow. A doorway led to a small room where another door revealed a stone stairway. They went down some way and it got quite dark before they went through another doorway into a larger chamber with openings above them, which allowed some light to filter in. Neither Teague nor Abbon could guess the purpose of this underground room but in one corner there was a large cage containing a rather sad looking animal. Abbon looked both elated and sad at once. The creature was indeed the simian that he was looking for, but Abbon sensed that something was not right. It was rocking back and forth, as though in great distress, like a child who has lost its mother. As they approached the cage, it flung itself at the bars in a screaming rage. Everyone stepped back involuntarily.

Abbon's voice came out in an involuntary hoarse whisper. "I need to find animals like this but in their natural place. Where do they come from?"

"I do not know," the priest admitted. "I only know that traders sometimes bring them here from a long way up the Nile. Far beyond Memphis, beyond Thebes, and even perhaps beyond Nubia," he trailed off.

Abbon looked away from the cage. Looking at the creature disturbed him. "How long would it take to travel to these lands?"

"Perhaps three moons to reach Ebou," he hesitated. "Or rather, it is called Elephantin in Hellenic. Three moons by boat up the river. It would take at least as long again to reach Meroe in the kingdom of Kush."

"How long to walk or ride beside the river?"

"Is the journey not slow enough and dangerous enough by river?" the priest asked in surprise.

Abbon thought for a moment and then said, "Well, it seems I will be gone for at least a year, Teague. But less time than your journey will take?"

"You have to find the creature and study it first, Brother. You travel to unknown lands and must avoid being killed by whichever people live in the places you visit."

"Ha! While it is true that I head into the unknown lands, there may not even be people beyond the land of Kush and the journey is shorter than yours. You must cross the entire Parthian empire on your quest, and we already know they are a proud warrior people. Even if you make it back, that torc is surely mine."

"We'll see, little brother," Teague retorted with a smile as he put the stress on the word 'little'.

Abbon ignored this as he remembered something else. "Oh, I need to know; by what name is this simian known?"

The priest looked worried. "I don't think there is a specific name for this type of simian."

"How will I ask people where to find it?" Abbon wondered aloud.

46

Crassus still hoped to avoid a straight fight against Spartacus. It was not a question of doubting his abilities, or those of his legions, but if he could end this rebellion without further bloodshed it would free up his troops for other campaigns. Furthermore, Roman politics was having an influence over his plans. Crassus, like all great Romans, needed success to build up his reputation; his auctoritas. The young general Pompey had more than his fair share of success already and now he was on his way to join Crassus. Should he arrive before Spartacus was defeated he would certainly take the greater share of the credit and Crassus would be overlooked.

Spartacus, hemmed into the peninsular unless he could reach Sicilia, aware of the news that Pompey was marching south through Italia, and therefore of the urgent need to come to terms before he faced two generals with twice the legions, was also willing to discuss terms, and so a truce was called. The meeting took place in an open field. Spartacus was accompanied by a small guard of twenty of his best men, as well as the new generals, Gannicus of the Arverni and Castus of the Rugii, who had naturally gravitated to replace Crixus and

Oenomaus. Both men had been taken as slaves when they were just children and had never known any other life, and yet somewhere deep in their bones there was a proud fierce warrior streak that had been displayed time and again against their hated Roman oppressors. Gwenn was there too, the mysterious woman about whom so many stories had already begun to be spun, the only one of which was true was that which was the least believable; that she had magical powers.

Crassus was flanked by a small guard of his best legionaries, and a select group of tribunes which, despite his still relatively junior position, included Gaius Julius Caesar. Caesar's dark eyes met Gwenn's ice blue in a look which conveyed a mixture of curiosity, anger, and superiority. Did she know that she had set herself against him, her patron? If so, how did she dare? Gwenn began to wonder if she was in fact fighting on the wrong side. She looked at Spartacus, who was outlining his demands. He wanted safe passage to Sicilia for his entire army. She looked at Caesar as she heard Crassus state in no uncertain terms that such a gift was not in his power, nor would he grant it if it were.

Caesar's eyes bored into her and she felt herself becoming weak again. She felt angry at her weakness, and the anger battled against it but made little headway. Did he know he had this power?

The words of Spartacus and Crassus seemed so far away: echoing and ethereal. She thought she heard Spartacus ask, at least, for the women and children to be allowed to leave Rome, though what use that would be to them with nobody to protect them in whatever lands they ended up in was a mystery to Gwenn. Either way, it seemed Crassus sought nothing less than complete capitulation from the entire slave army. A return to servitude and certainly in the worst possible conditions, mining for the strongest fighters, agricultural work on the latifunda for the women and children. Crassus was offering Spartacus a death sentence for the entire slave army and all their retinue. The only difference it seemed was that if Spartacus did not agree, then the execution would be swift at the point of a gladius, while if he did, it would be lingering over many months or years of back breaking toil.

Spartacus, enraged, refused Crassus' impossible terms and the two parties withdrew, watchful, mistrusting, and angry. This broke the spell that held Gwenn, and she too returned with Spartacus to the main body of the army. She had not exchanged a single word with Caesar, but she felt unable to think or decide what her next course of action should be. Spartacus was issuing orders. Pompey was heading south while they were trapped in the tip of the peninsula but, if they broke out, they could head towards Brundisium, capture the town and defend it from there while they awaited ships to take them away. Gwenn sought out Epona at the first opportunity.

"I can't fight him."

Epona poured wine and listened, saying nothing.

Gwenn gulped down a mouthful of unwatered wine and repeated herself. "I can't fight him, Epona.

He's… he has some power over me that no man could ever have. He just looked at me and I lost control over my own thoughts. I think, for a moment I wanted to leave all this behind and just become his slave again." Her head dropped into her hands in a gesture of complete capitulation.

Epona sat silently, waiting to see if there was anything more. There wasn't.

"We should leave here. Just get right away. Crixus is dead, I know it's ridiculous, but I actually imagined spending the rest of my life with him, back in my old home among the Iceni, or anywhere away from Rome and Romans. There's nothing for me here now and nothing for you either. Don't give me that look; he's a man, *just* a man, nothing more. Not a powerful mage, and certainly of no interest to you except for this kharisma that he has over you that he doesn't even know he has. No, not really. He knows he has some power over you, but he doesn't understand it. The further away from him you are the better."

Gwenn looked beseechingly at her friend but said nothing.

"Didn't you say there was a woman at Brigantio beyond the Alps? What was her name?"

"Glaessa," Gwenn muttered, adding, "the amber mage."

Gwenn's face took on a slightly more serene look as she remembered Glaessa, her green eyes and copper hair glinting in the sunlight. Then she looked directly at Epona.

"But how can we abandon these people now, after all we've been through? The Romani will destroy them, one way or another."

"That's the problem. One way or another. What can we do, you and I? Two women in a fight between thousands of men. How many minds can you control at once?"

"None if Caesar's is one of them."

"So do we stay and see this through to the bitter end, or leave now and get as far away as possible?"

Gwenn set her jaw and stood up. At her full height she was at least a foot taller than her friend.

"We stay, we try to mitigate the worst that Rome can do. Perhaps we can get some of the slaves away to safety? We have to try."

"Agreed," Epona said, and she poured more wine to drink to their decision.

"Just keep well away from Caesar," she added as she drained the cup.

47

Despite all the efforts of Crassus to stockade the Spartacani in the peninsula, despite the ditch and wall, and troops stationed along it at regular intervals, Spartacus performed another miraculous escape. As winter snows fell, lending silence to their footsteps, the slave army bridged one of the weaker points of the wall using vast numbers of branches and all passed safely through the Roman lines in the night.

The plan now was to head for Brundisium, and the army marched north through Regium at a fast pace. Crassus was furious when he found out they had escaped his trap and gave pursuit. His reputation depended absolutely on being able to destroy Spartacus before Pompey arrived to take all the glory. News came now of another Roman force coming from Macedonia and landing at Brundisium, thereby restricting Spartacus still further.

Discipline, already minimal in the slave army, began to break down completely as small factions broke off from the main body and engaged with Crassus' legions. Some fared well, most badly. Gannicus and Castus took a large force of mostly Gallic and Germanic slaves and were met by some six thousand legionaries, led by two of Crassus' commanders, Lucius Pomptinus and Quintus Marcius Rufus. Despite having nearly twice that number of men, both Gannicus and Castus died along with almost their entire force. When news got back to Spartacus he knew this was the beginning of the end. There was no escape, and no possibility of victory; only the hope of an honourable death and perhaps to become immortalised in stories.

Not that he relayed this hopeless situation to the men under his command. Before the final battle he spoke to the massed ranks of slaves, farmers, and Italian tribesmen who had destroyed every army that Rome had thrown at them until now. He told them how, over a hundred years before, almost in the same place that they would do battle, a great general named Hannibal had utterly destroyed a vastly superior Roman army. He told them that they too would, through cunning, and bravery, and the blessings of the Gods, destroy the legions of Marcus Licinius Crassus, and then they would turn upon Pompey and destroy him too. He swore that by the end of the year they would march into Rome and they would free all slaves and enslave the Romans instead. It was stirring stuff, delivered with confidence and bravado. It raised a cheer and the sound of swords beating against shields became deafening.

When the fighting began, it almost seemed as though his optimistic prophesies might actually turn out to be true. Ten legions took to the field, some forty thousand men, largely consisting of regular legionaries but also with supporting cavalry. The slave army included a number of archers and slingers who rained down volleys or missiles on the advancing legions, who appeared to become bogged down and unable to press forward. They were, however, forming tight formations until the initial ranged attacks slowed as the archers ran low on ammunition. When they did advance, the slave army lines quickly broke and the more experienced and disciplined tactics of the legions began to make themselves felt.

Once again, both Gwenn and Epona were away from the thick of the fighting, having chosen an elevated position on a hillside to the west, overlooking the valley of the Silarius river where the fighting was taking place. They could only watch as the slave army was being destroyed in that savagely methodical way that Roman legions employed to propel them to victory against less disciplined enemies. The smash of the shield into face and body, the surgical thrust of the gladius finding a gap in the defences and slicing into flesh, and then moving on to the next, and the next. The tight formation with shields touching and, on the command from the centurion, the front rank would fall back leaving the next rank to take over, smash, stab, smash, stab, until they too would move back leaving the next rank, and the next, always keeping the freshest troops at the point of contact with the enemy. When it worked, it was devastating. It depended on the army being absolutely disciplined and loyal, and that effect Crassus had achieved when he had ordered the decimation. Death in battle held no fear when compared with the possibility of death at the hands of your own comrades. There were a few more volleys of arrows from archers, and shot from slingers but, by now, in the milling mob of fighters, these attacks were as deadly to the slave army as they were to the legions.

Epona couldn't see Spartacus, but she knew that somewhere in the hideous, churning, monstrous scene below her he would be fighting for his life: fighting to the death. He would give no mercy, nor ask for it. While the legionary feared decimation above death in battle, Spartacus feared the humiliation and agonising death that he knew awaited him if he were captured. Unseen by Gwenn or Epona, unnoticed even by those around him who were also engaged in their own struggles, Spartacus had one intent. To kill Crassus. He slashed and fought his way through lines of ordinary legionaries; his overwhelming strength and skill, combined with fierce passion, drove him forward until he was within sight of the Roman general. He even managed to kill or fatally wound some of the general's personal guard, but the force that had brought him to this point began to run out. He parried and slashed and beat away attack after attack with his shield and sword, until a spear found his thigh and was embedded in the dense muscles. It dragged him sideways, unbalancing him as he continued to slash wildly, surrounded. Somehow he was given enough space and time to pull the weapon out with teeth gritted against the pain. Blood ran freely down his leg from the gaping wound as, desperately, brutishly, he lunged forwards slashing and parrying despite the agony and the overwhelming odds. Finally, a gladius found a gap and pierced his side. Having already lost a lot of blood this final blow was too much. Spartacus' body slumped as the injured leg collapsed beneath him.

Both Gwenn and Epona knew this was the end. They were close enough to the edge of the fighting to fire slingshots into the melee, but there was no guarantee who they might hit. Epona was crying, Gwenn stony faced, lost in thought. At that moment a stray arrow struck Epona in the face. Gwenn watched Epona stagger backwards, seemingly in slow motion. Gwenn could hear screaming as she watched Epona fall and then roll down the slope, stopped by a tangle of bushes. It was a few moments before Gwenn realised the screaming was coming from her own mouth. As she dashed down the slope to try to help her friend she already knew there would be nothing she could do.

48

A young man in a boat sailing up the Nile felt a sudden stab of homesickness, and a dark depression hung over him like a cloud for no reason he could explain. His brother, on a ship from Alexandria to Tyrus, felt a similar pang. He described it to a passing sailor, who noticed him suddenly wince in apparent pain, as feeling like a fishing hook had just been pulled out of his stomach. He, too, felt a wrenching, gnawing feeling that lasted for several days, but couldn't explain why.

Far to the north, the eldest brother felt it the strongest of all. He was gazing out over a frozen lake watching a distant pack of wolves picking their way between sparse conifers covered with snow when the black feeling descended upon him again; the empty, stomach churning, hopeless darkness of the khaos before the beginning of time, before the earth and the sky were formed. He did not know the reason for this feeling, only that it was as real as the slash of a sword, or the stab of a spear. There was a gnawing pain like an intense hunger of the soul and Blyth fell to his knees and wept, then transformed into a wolf and howled an ethereal and mournful howl that echoed on and on into the evening sky.

Elarch felt it too, although less intensely; just an inexplicable sense of dread and foreboding.

Only Kaito, sitting talking to Blodwyth in the house which they had built beside the little farmstead of Biarni, recognised the source of the pain which, for him, was less terrible. It was more like a dull ache, as though he felt it indirectly; as though he were feeling the pain of Blyth, Teague, Abbon, and Elarch second-hand, but combined into one.

"Something terrible has happened to Epona," he told Blodwyth.

"What?"

They heard the howl of a wolf, ghostly and pitiful, which cut through the crackling flames.

"I don't know, but I think she may even have been killed."

Blodwyth gasped while Kaito stood up and went to a table where he opened a wax tablet. He scratched a series of short parallel lines, some vertical, some horizontal, a few at angles or crossing. Blodwyth knew the writing system and was able to read, "Epona, what happened?"

She could feel her heart pounding in her chest as she watched and waited. It seemed eternity before the words began to fade from the surface of the wax and were replaced by a similar series of lines which conveyed the message nobody wanted to read.

Kaito put on his cloak, took his staff and said, "I have to find Blyth."

Blodwyth was left with her thoughts, which were interrupted by Kallon who woke and began to cry.

Outside it was already night; the land was blanketed in white faded to dark blue in the moonlight, as far as the eye could see. Kaito looked as though he was sniffing the air. A distant wolf howled. He moved almost too swiftly for such an ancient man. Then in the space of a few paces, the man disappeared, becoming a snow-white bird that flapped silently a few times and then soared into the deep blue-grey sky. The old man had not wasted his time while living in this place and had reason to be glad of the new transformations he had learned.

49

Gwenn carried Epona's body higher up the hillside away from the ebbing carnage below, seemingly ignoring the dead weight in her arms she climbed to the ridge and beyond. The sun was setting as she laid Epona's body down in a clear rocky spot, where she could build a funeral pyre, and began gathering firewood.

Bitter anger rose inside her as she hacked mercilessly at saplings and dragged fallen branches together in a heap. It took a considerable time and the almost full moon had risen before she was ready to perform the rites that would send her friend to the halls of Lugh. It wasn't how she would have hoped to send her. Indeed, she thought she would sooner it had been her lying there, serene, and free of the burdens of life, while Epona had to gather firewood and prepare her body. She shook her head, to clear the selfish thoughts, and pointed her staff at the pyre.

Gwenn stood motionless, watching the flames engulf the body. She didn't move even when smoke blew into her eyes and made them stream, even when the heat got too much and felt like it was burning her too. She cried, great wracking, heaving, rending sobs, and she scratched her arms until the skin bled. The stench of burning flesh was masked by the oils she had poured over the body, giving off a heady sweet vapour. The scent somehow recalled every funeral Gwenn had attended. She realised there had been too many. Eventually she sat down, careless of where she was or even if she were safe. The flames continued for a long time, slowly burning down to embers and Gwenn slept until the warmth from the flames was no longer enough to keep out the cold of the winter night.

Somehow, despite her proximity to the site of the battle and her complete lack of security during the night, she had remained undisturbed. The silence was intense. She looked at the stars. The moon was no longer visible in the sky, and she thought she could see a hint of the new dawn colouring the eastern horizon. She knew the battle had gone as badly as it was possible for it to go. Spartacus was dead, along with… She couldn't even say for sure how many men had fought.

She started at a sound of movement and ducked into the sparse undergrowth. There was little enough cover here before she had built a funeral pyre. Keeping painfully still she waited, scarcely breathing. There was a long gentle slope directly in front, another slightly steeper coming up from the river valley, and another similar one going down the other side to the next dip in the land. Some distance behind her, she was aware of a steeper drop where the ground was highest and fell away for a considerable distance. Whoever was coming they were ahead of her on the shallower slope.

From the roughly cobbled together armour and curved sword, she deduced it was one of the slave army who had, presumably, escaped though not, she noticed, without taking some damage. He was limping, and blood had caked around a gash in his left thigh. She didn't recognise him, but she stood anyway. He started, like a hare that has stumbled out of the woods into the hunter.

"I mean you no harm," she said quickly.

His hand moved away from the sword hilt as he visibly relaxed, recognising her immediately.

"We were annihilated."

"I know. Here, let me see to that wound."

"What's the point? They are searching for the survivors. No sense patching me up just so they can put me in the arena for their entertainment."

"Hope is the gift of the living."

The weary fighter, observing her serene expression, wondered if she had any idea what he had just been through, watching his friends die, but he said nothing and allowed her to tend his wound.

"So how bad is it?" she asked, cleaning the wound expertly.

He winced and answered, "It is as bad as it can possibly be. Spartacus is dead."

She ripped some clean fabric and began to tie it.

"I know. How many others lost?"

"It's hard to say for sure. Perhaps two legions of our men escaped the field? We made no impact on them beyond a few thousand Romans dead in the early exchanges."

Gwenn tied the bandage as she thought of the enormity of the loss. Two legions remained, and those scattered across the countryside being hunted down by a dozen legions of veteran Roman soldiers. There was nowhere left to run, and nowhere to hide. All those who would have joined Spartacus had done so in the previous year. She wondered if some might be able to melt back into society. Those who had been freemen of Italian tribes, perhaps: slaves surely not. The man looked straight at her from haunted greyish-brown eyes.

"You know there will be no mercy, don't you? Don't let them capture you alive. Sooner a gladius between the ribs than whatever gruesome end they have planned for us."

"Come on, let's see if we can get away from here without being seen." She offered the fighter a hand to get up, but he was scarcely on his feet when they heard a shout from down the slope.

"Two more up here!"

A legionary was approaching and several more emerged not far behind. The slave fighter drew his curved sword and stepped in front of Gwenn.

"We can't fight them. Let's try our luck on the steeper slope!" Gwenn hissed.

"Do what you have to do. I'll go down fighting."

He squared up to the advancing legionaries. The first pilum missed, landing in the hard-packed soil and rock, the point bending beyond use so that it could not be thrown back. The second was on target but the fighter's reflexes were enough to raise his shield and deflect the weapon. More legionaries appeared and more javelins were thrown, one finally finding its mark.

"I said there was no point fixing me up," he was able to call back as he fell to his knees. "Remember, don't let them catch you alive."

Gwenn didn't have time to mourn as the slave fighter was ruthlessly cut down, thus finishing what the pilum had begun, and the remaining legionaries advanced on her. Two more javelins sailed past her as she ran headlong up the slope to the steepest part of the drop. Against the expectations of the pursuing soldiers she didn't stop but launched herself off the edge to certain death below.

50

Looking down over the snow dusted ground the snowy owl rode on the faintest of thermals in the crackling-cold air, beating its wings minimally to keep aloft and change direction. Its keen eyes scanned the soft bluish-white, faintly undulating, terrain in search of a darker shape. There was a wolf pack, winding along, leaving a trail through the most recent snowfall, but he was seeking out a dark, lone wolf which would be more difficult to spot. But he had one major advantage. He could *feel* the right direction to fly. He swooshed over a dense stand of trees and sensed he had overshot his mark. Landing in the branches of a spruce tree, with the inexpert clumsiness of a human ill-used to occupying the form of a bird, he regained his composure and looked down.

Blyth stood on four paws with no purpose or goal in mind. While he took on the shape of the wolf he found there was less room in his mind for the awful feelings that washed over him in his human form. But still the dull, twisting, bitter ache filled his thoughts; he wanted to run from it, but it was inside him and he couldn't move, felt no reason to move. He thought bitterly of the saying, 'hope is the gift of the living', and wondered if that meant he was already dead. An owl landed in front of him. A real wolf would probably have prepared to pounce. Blyth watched it listlessly as it transformed into Kaito. The wolf remained motionless.

"Blyth. Come with me."

The wolf bristled but made no attempt to leave or to follow. Kaito moved forward. Unconsciously, Blyth raised his hackles and bared long sharp fangs. Kaito put his hand out, gently, seeking contact. The wolf lunged at the man, who snapped seemingly out of existence. A faint buzzing moved behind Blyth and then Kaito reappeared. Blyth turned and snapped again but again the mage snapped out of existence and with a brief buzz appeared again at another point.

"How long do you intend to stay as a wolf, Blyth? Forever? I think I can help you but not like this."

The wolf lunged again but this time was met with another wolf, smaller, but more than a match in agility. Blyth rolled over in the snow having missed his attack. When he stood up, the other wolf was gone and Kaito was there, serene and calm, as though this fight was costing him nothing in terms of effort. The dark empty void in Blyth's mind was filled with burning rage. He lunged again, and this time Kaito changed and exploded upwards in a flurry of white wings. The owl alighted in the branch of a tree higher than the wolf could jump although Blyth tried, nevertheless.

The owl changed again, into a squirrel. It was not the usual reddish copper, nor the often seen dark brown almost black, but instead an almost impossible white colour. It flicked its bushy tail provocatively and scampered along the branch, launching into the air and skittering across the snow-covered ground to the next tree where it surged up the trunk with the enraged wolf close on its tail. It was still night, bitterly cold and dark. Kaito had three things he needed to do before he could help Blyth. He needed him back at the farmstead, he needed him in his human form, and he desperately needed him to want help. At the moment, it seemed none of these things was the case. But Blyth was enraged, and the emotion filled the void in him, at least for now, and it also gave Kaito a way to get him home.

The owl swooped low over the land, alighting a few hundred yards ahead. The wolf stalked it, snarling, then leapt and raced snapping its jaws closed on the place where the owl had been moments before. The squirrel once again skittered along the ground before launching up onto silky silent wings just ahead of the wolf's powerful jaws. The more he failed, the more Blyth wanted to hurt this shifting switching creature, even though deep in his subconscious he also knew it was Kaito who was doing this to him. The wolf mind saw the hunt and instinctively chased the movement, while Blyth's human mind was largely devoid of emotions beyond burning rage.

As he chased again, an unexpected slip by Kaito in squirrel form saw the wolf's teeth snap shut on the white fluffy tail. It disappeared again and in the darkness a faint buzzing continued onwards and upwards. The wolf followed instinctively as, in the dark sky, the white owl emerged with a flurry of feathers and flapped its wings, leisurely riding the breeze. Anger made a little room for curiosity. Blyth couldn't help but wonder where Kaito went when he disappeared like that. He followed the owl, which now looped slowly over the landscape, feeling with his mind to be sure Blyth was following.

After an hour or so of travelling like this, the owl landed a few hundred paces ahead and transformed once again into Kaito. He felt tired but did not show it outwardly. He turned and looked back at the wolf. The wolf hesitated, and after a long pause eventually turned back into Blyth. He stood looking at the farmstead just visible over the crest of the next rise. It was cold. Blyth thought about his son, and about Blodwyth. It was the first time since he had transformed that he had held a thought in his head about anything that really mattered.

He shivered in the biting cold and thought now of Kaito. Why had he come out on a freezing winter night for him? Kaito the Wise Oak, how old was he again? A good deal more than one hundred winters, Blyth knew. Competing for attention in Blyth's troubled mind now were rage, curiosity, and guilt. None of them were particularly positive emotions, but they were emotions, nonetheless. He quickened his pace, but his expression remained troubled. Whatever his feelings, he followed the old mage into their house.

51

Gwenn's wings lifted her easily on morning thermals pushing up the slope; she lingered long enough to watch the legionaries look over the edge in search of her mangled body. She wondered if they would climb down or make a note and return to the spot later. It didn't matter really, but she felt too bitter to feel much pleasure from this small victory. The situation seemed hopeless. From high above, through the eyes of an eagle, she saw small bands of slave fighters rounded up and either killed fighting back or captured and dragged away by the overwhelming numbers of Roman soldiers.

She flew over the legionary camps and command tents looking, looking; she didn't admit to herself that she was looking for Caesar. In all this carnage, she somehow clung to the idea that her Caesar was different, that he was kinder, more just, a man who respected different cultures and peoples. Hadn't he learned to speak several tribal dialects of Gallic? His servants idolised him. She recalled that they would have laid down their lives for him. Caesar even treated women with respect, a rare enough thing even among Gallic tribes and almost unheard of in her experience of Romans.

She couldn't see him, but she saw Crassus, the general who had forced his own men to kill each other as punishment for running away. Crassus, whose legions had crushed Spartacus and the last hope of freedom for thousands of oppressed people. She wanted to hate him, but she knew that hate would burn you up from the inside and there was nothing she could do anyway.

She saw one small contingent of the slave army, their number equivalent to a legion. They were headed north when they encountered Pompey's legions moving south. None survived. The Romani had won and that was the end of it. What had Epona told her? She should leave here and go back to Glaessa. The eagle jolted slightly in the air as Gwenn momentarily lost control of her aquiline wings at the thought of Glaessa, her copper hair shining like a newly-cast brooch, and her body warm against cold nights. But she could not leave yet. She had to see what happened next.

The captured slaves were tied together and marched at a rapid pace, northwards, towards Capua and Rome, reaching Capua in two days. From there the legionaries turned their activity towards construction once more. Some were engaged in digging pits some two feet square and several feet deep. Others cut trees down, the trunks being dragged to the roadside.

On the following day she began to have a clear idea of what Crassus had planned as she saw the first posts being dropped into the holes at regular intervals along the roadside. She realised as she flew north along the Via Appia that these holes were being dug all the way along the road at intervals of some thirty paces between each one. It wasn't possible to count their number. Gwenn's head spun as she flew back towards Capua and saw the first slaves being tied up to the posts. She had to land and transform into her human form if only to allow her to be violently sick. She remembered Caesar overseeing the building of six hundred crucifixion posts. But that had been for pirates who had captured him and demanded a ransom. They had killed and tortured people purely to get rich and had Caesar not captured them they would have continued to do so at will for a long time to come. Caesar had been merciful too. He had slit their throats soon after tying them up, rather than leave them to die days later of thirst or hunger.

The style of post varied despite the regimented process of constructing them. Initially the posts had a crossbar over which the arms of the victims were hung and tied down. But as the posts were being made, hurriedly, from available materials they became simpler with the victim's wrists simply tied to a protruding branch near the top with a supporting block under the feet, or between the legs. In many places there was a suitable tree already in about the right place, and to this the victim was tied fast to the branches. There was to be no merciful throat slitting for these rebellious slaves. It was a busy road with merchants and travellers heading in both directions throughout the daylight hours. In some cases, depending on the whim of those involved, there might also be nails driven through the wrists or feet, although this was largely unnecessary and done out of spite and when nails were available to hand.

Crassus had good reasons of his own to keep his legions prepared for fighting but, for now, he was happy for them to guard the endless lines of dying rebels, day and night, along the whole length of the road from Capua to Rome, some four days' march in all, and at every thirty paces another hideously hopeless figure. Some, arguably the lucky ones, slipped from their foot supports leaving the full weight of their body hanging from their arms. Those with their arms tied directly above them very quickly found it harder and harder to draw air into their lungs and were dead within ten minutes of the drop. Those whose arms were tied to a cross beam, or to tree branches, lasted longer but once their weight was entirely on their arms the end came by the following day.

Gwenn, bitterly, choked on the words she had said to the man whose wounds she had dressed days before – only to see him cut down moments later.

'Hope is the gift of the living,' she had said. What hope was there but for the mercy of death? She flew closer, not daring to appear in human form before the endless lines of legionaries taking turns on guard duty. Some men had wounds inflicted in battle, still left untreated. Others - most actually - had additional wounds inflicted as part of the process of crucifixion, these depending on the vindictiveness of their captors. Many bled out, slowly but surely. Others, whose wounds had scabbed over, suffered a worse fate as these turned septic, the skin turned black, and green pus oozed, which attracted the interest of early flies as the worst of winter gave way to spring. Flies and other insects landed on the victims in greater numbers, not only to feed on the open wounds but also to take advantage of the moisture in their sweat, or to stab through the skin and draw blood. There was nothing they could do but twist a head until they no longer had strength for even this small exertion.

The hardiest, whose method of tying and supporting had been conducted in such a way as to prevent asphyxiation, and whose wounds were not unduly serious, lasted for several days. Their skin dried out; no longer able to sweat they burned in the early spring sun and froze in the cold nights. Too weak to support their heads, they died one by one in the most unbearable agony.

Gwenn had no tears left to shed and was fighting off the urge to hate without limits. She knew she would leave Rome and hoped she would never return.

A golden eagle took off from a high tree overlooking the Via Appia and soared north, beyond Rome, before landing and becoming once again the warrior mage, Gwenn. She set her eyes on the distant horizon and began walking.

52

It was still dark in the far north, although the line of sky above the horizon was slowly shifting from black through deep blue to a pale green the colour of a shallow, clear sea. Blyth struggled with his emotions until curiosity won.

"How do you do that...thing? The disappearing trick?"

"I can't tell you, Blyth. Not yet in any case. It is far too dangerous, for now."

'For now?' thought Blyth, 'so I may learn yet?' The nagging doubts flooded back. His anger had subsided, his guilt forgotten, as the old man warmed by the fire and poured hot water into a cup, and the curiosity was not strong enough alone to hold back the feelings of worthlessness and futility that had been engulfing him again. He knew, deep down, that whatever he had felt yesterday, that painful wrench, was bad news; but also he knew that it was not the trigger for his descent into the black khaos that had engulfed him. He had been feeling it more strongly for some time; how long he could not say. When he had found Blodwyth, they had agreed that they should all stay there rather than travel with Kallon being so young. He was growing quickly and was already walking and playing. He adored Kaito, and Blyth wondered idly if he would ever realise how extraordinary it was for a child to be able to play with the father of his father's, father's… he felt at his fingers, counting up, and then realised how silly he was being. He spoke again.

"Too dangerous? Why does it matter anyway?"

"And your second question answers the first. Transformations are always dangerous, but more so for one who is troubled and not calm. You appear not to value your own life."

"My life is worthless."

"There are those who think otherwise." Kaito glanced at Kallon, who was sleeping soundly.

"I should never have brought him to this world."

"The Gods did that. You were just a messenger, Blodwyth the vessel."

"The Gods hate me too."

"I doubt it. I do not believe they consider any of us at all. Either to hate or to love. We are like the pieces in a game to them."

"Is that supposed to make me feel better?"

"No."

There was a lengthy silence before Kaito spoke again.

"Tell me, in as much detail as you can, what feelings you endure when you have your dark periods, and remember, I have been through it all myself, so don't worry about sounding ridiculous."

Blyth sighed deeply. The last thing he felt he wanted to do was to describe his feelings in detail, even to a man who had experienced many of the same things, but somehow he dredged some words up and began to talk. Kaito said nothing but nodded imperceptibly as he listened, never once taking his eyes off the young man in front of him.

"For one thing, I often don't *feel* anything at all. It's just emptiness. I said before about the state of being before time existed, before the heavens and the earth existed; the time of Khaos? It's not a feeling that can be described, or understood as a feeling, but more of an empty blackness, swirling and confused. Yet, within that khaos there are forms. There is a feeling of oppressive weight pushing me down, holding me down, as though a horse has fallen on top of me and now won't get up. It's not dead but it is actively trying to pin me down. Like fighting a huge bear, and every slash of the sword only makes the bear's skin tougher, until the bear is made of iron and its paws contain rows of swords, and it slashes but only makes tiny cuts; hundreds and hundreds of tiny cuts and the pain feels good because it is a feeling.

"Often I can't eat; there is food, but I can't taste it, and I don't want to let it pass my lips. I have no desire to drink either. If I could stop up my nose and mouth I would. When I was on that boat, I longed to fall overboard and drown in the deep waters, but I couldn't even bring myself to get up on deck, much less climb over the edge and slip away. I didn't know where I was or why I was there. I felt like that last night too. As the wolf, I lose some of the pain and confusion. There's less room in its mind to hold all that terror, but there is less room to deal with it either. I don't want to feel like this, I don't want to be useless and worthless. Even if it is only for my son, I want to be able to control it; I would give up every bit of my magical gift in a second if I could just never feel like I do right now."

While Blyth was speaking Kaito, still watching and listening intently, filled a cup with boiling water and let it cool for a minute before pouring the water into another cup. When Blyth had finished speaking the old man stood up and said, "If you will come with me, I may have something that can help."

"I'm willing to try," Blyth muttered.

Kaito picked up a bag, and the cup which contained some sort of brown, muddy liquid. He led the way out of the house and across the snowy landscape to a small clearing among tall looming spruce, pine, and larch, overlooking the lake to the east. The sun was just about to crest the horizon and there was a broad band of pale green in the sky there.

Kaito drew a large circle with his staff and handed Blyth the cup.

"This tastes disgusting, and it will make you feel very strange for a while, but it may also help remove the worst of the Gods' curse."

Blyth took the cup while Kaito pulled together a small fire from fallen branches and twigs. He lit it with a wave of his staff. Blyth looked at the muddy, brown brew. Eventually he drank some. It did indeed taste revolting, but Blyth had already implied he would cheerfully discard his magic, or accept physical pain, or even death, sooner than experience the feeling of khaos again, so drinking one cup of filthy water that tasted like muddy tea was a small price to pay.

Blyth grimaced and lifted the cup, but Kaito gently put out a hand and said, "Take small sips, and wait between each until you begin to feel the effects."

"What are the effects?" Blyth asked, as he took another sip.

"They vary, but you will know. If you give me permission I will dip into your mind to try to work out if you have drunk enough."

"You have my permission." Blyth took another sip. It took a while for anything unusual to happen.

Blyth watched as Bellenos appeared on the horizon and rose slowly in a haze of vivid orange. Gradually the light began to burst into a display of colours as vibrant as any sunrise Blyth had seen. At first it was a blend of red through yellow with wisps of blue smeared through, then the colours began to move and shift, and into the blend there were swirls of purple and green. Small stars burst into existence and winked out. Kaito, inside Blyth's mind, could see the effect too and he gently took the cup from Blyth's unprotesting hand and poured the remaining liquid away. Blyth turned to Kaito who was glowing slightly, his rich blue cloak seemingly reflecting the sunrise in swirls of dancing colours, the fire flickering in the centre of the circle appeared filled with naked dancing figures, their orange and yellow bodies writhing sensuously and rhythmically. Blyth laughed like a child playing with its parents. Although he was standing still, he felt as though he was running through green fields of long grass, studded with buttercups and daisies. As he ran he felt light; lighter than air. He felt his body leave the ground and he soared over the landscape, all the while the sunrise dancing and exploding in every colour of the rainbow, rippling, shifting, separating, and merging, in wildly criss-crossing patterns like the most intricate knots. The knots were tied from multicoloured snakes that writhed and hissed menacingly. The fire dancers turned angry faces towards him, and he started backwards in horror. Kaito turned to him, his blue cloak glowing in an ethereal light, and pulled back his hood revealing a bare white skull where his face should be.

Seeing the experience going badly wrong for Blyth, Kaito gently touched a few strands of his thoughts and the hideous visons faded. Instead of a skull, there was Kaito's smiling wrinkled face, the eyes twinkling. Blyth felt the dark pupils of those eyes growing larger before him as he drifted towards them, they became as large as the night sky enveloping him, the little white glint in the corner became a star, and then thousands of stars, and he was floating among them, smiling contentedly. It seemed a long time that he floated there before slowly drifting down again. Kaito's face reformed, smiling but not so vibrant now, the sunrise was gone and the yellow orb of Bellenos was higher in the sky, the fire was crackling merrily but no longer contained the naked dancers. He felt Kaito leave his mind and the ordinary everyday sounds and smells came rushing back, their absence unnoticed until they had returned; he knew somehow they would fade into the background again soon enough.

He looked at Kaito and whispered, "Oh!"

Kaito nodded and smiled but said nothing. With a wave of his staff the circle in which he had deliberately enclosed them to keep Blyth safe vanished, and he led the way back to the house.

53

It took almost a full moon cycle for Gwenn to travel from Rome to Brigantio, avoiding changing into animal form as far as possible. She sensed that she had spent too long as an eagle and had almost failed to change back.

There were a few tense occasions when she spotted soldiers too late and had to walk past as though she was just a perfectly innocent woman walking northwards through Italia. Six feet tall, Gwenn was not a woman you forgot seeing. She could console herself that these men were unlikely to belong to Crassus but were more likely to be from Pompey's legions and had therefore not been involved in the fighting. They could scarcely be expected to have seen or known about her involvement.

On her way to the Alps she made sure she passed through Mediolanum. It wasn't really a detour and she wanted to visit the family of a man she had tried to help some years earlier. Alios had been very ill, but the advice she had given him, if followed closely, would almost certainly ensure his full recovery. On approaching the farm she could see a ploughman, with a pair of oxen, ploughing the field. Drawing closer she could clearly see

Alios, with his son, now very much taller, leading the cattle. The last time she had been there she had seen Alios bent double in agony with an affliction of the Gods. Now, he was ruddy faced in the spring sunshine walking behind the plough and showing all the signs of being completely well again. Intent on keeping a straight furrow, he didn't notice Gwenn until she was almost next to him. When he did see her, his face exploded into an ecstatic grin.

"Hi-hi-hi!" he called to the oxen, pulling back on the guide rope. The great beasts needed little encouragement to rest, their black hides flecked with sweat, plagued by flies, and steaming from the combination of spring sunshine and body heat.

The lad at the front stopped too and looked at Gwenn. He had been a young boy, only old enough to help with the simplest of chores like collecting firewood or sweeping and cleaning, when she had last passed through. Now he was a strapping young man, perhaps already with a woman, or at least with one in mind. His memory of Gwenn was hazy at best, but the family often spoke of the strange mage-woman who had removed the Gods' curse from their father, and he smiled in gratitude for that. Alios was in a torment. He needed to finish the job of ploughing the field, which would likely take several more hours, but he also wanted to show Gwenn the best hospitality he could.

Gwenn saw his discomfort and said, "The Gods will not wait for you to plough this field, but I will."

Alios looked relieved, yet still uncomfortable. He decided he could afford to release his son for a while.

"Lugos, run back to the house and tell mother Gwenn is here. Then get straight back here, and we'll finish this field as quickly as possible."

Lugos dashed away and his father called after him, "Oh, and tell her to kill the fattest chicken and prepare it for the table!"

"Not on my account I hope," Gwenn quickly interjected. I don't eat meat or fowl except in extreme circumstances."

He called, louder this time, to the receding Lugos, "Forget the chicken! Just tell her Gwenn is here."

With that, he turned back to the plough. The oxen however seemed unwilling to move. He could either go in front of the plough to coax them forwards, or behind it to push it down into the hard-packed soil to dig the furrow. He could not manage both. Without asking, Gwenn took up a position at the front of the plough and gently clucked with her tongue at the two great wild-eyed beasts, coaxing them forward with renewed vigour.

"Well I'll be…" Alios smiled and set to his task once more.

They had finished the row and were on the return before Lugos came running back, breathless, with his younger sister and mother in tow. Everyone wanted to greet Gwenn who was now masterfully leading the oxen at a swift yet steady pace.

"Is there no task that you cannot perform better than a man?" Alios' wife exclaimed with an amused laugh.

"None I feel the need to attempt," Gwenn replied, grinning back.

She stepped away from the plough to allow Lugos back to his post and the two women walked back to the house, leaving the men to finish. After the horrors she had witnessed, the simple pleasures of assessing provisions and thinking about what additional foods might be growing nearby at this season to enhance their diet was an immense pleasure.

Alios' wife chattered amicably about a range of topics, in particular giving Gwenn assurances that Alios still ate meat only at the full, half, and new moons, and that they sacrificed a glass of fine wine every day to the Gods, just as Gwenn had ordered. At first, she said, Alios had hated the regime and complained that the porridge was dull and tasteless, but she had been determined he would stick to it and after a few moons he had got used to it and actually preferred simpler foods. He recovered from the Gods' curse but then found he felt better than he had before it had started.

Later, Gwenn enjoyed a meal with the whole family. The daughter was now a full-grown young woman and, Gwenn could tell, was in the early stages of becoming a mother herself, although Gwenn did not raise the subject.

On the following day Gwenn departed, amid fond farewells, and started for the mountains. She remained in human form until she reached the snowline and then transformed into the eagle to speed up the crossing and to reach Glaessa that much sooner.

54

Blyth longed to experience the exhilaration of the vibrant colours and the feeling of elation that he had just been through. He put the more unpleasant aspects of it to the back of his mind and recalled the euphoria that he felt, as though he were in the presence of Lugh, the shining one, himself. For a fleeting moment he wondered if Kaito was in fact a god. He dismissed the thought. It was as ridiculous as the idea that his mother, Epona, was in fact the goddess after whom she had been named.

"What was in that infusion?" he asked.

Kaito bore a blank face, neither stern nor smiling.

"It is too early to tell you, but I will soon. It was a powerful medicine which enters your spirit and opens up pathways to the Gods that are normally closed off. I can't explain it any better than that because... Well, because neither I nor anybody else understands it any better than that, if I am honest. The Gods blessed you and cursed you in equal measure, just as they did your father, and his father, and indeed myself and my father before me. No doubt this curse will pass again to Kallon and to every generation until the end of the world. And each generation will deal with it in their own way."

"You never told me what happened to my grandfather."

"You never asked."

"I think I didn't want to burden you with the memories so soon after my own father died. There has never been a good time to ask, it seems"

"Indeed, there never has. But the subject has come up and so I think I must discuss it. Trethiwr's father transformed into a bird."

Blyth's mind imagined any number of birds. An owl or an eagle, perhaps, or a swan, or a magpie. He had considered all of these, once he had learned to appreciate the benefits of transformations.

Kaito went on, "He spent a very long and arduous time watching a particular seabird; one with a pale body, a black head, and a red beak. It goes by many names, including 'tarrack' after the sound it makes. You will certainly have seen them at Ynys Mona where they gather is large numbers to breed. Unlike many seabirds they nest on flat ground, rather than cliff faces, but they will attack people in large numbers if disturbed. My son received many small cuts before he had studied them sufficiently. Almost as soon as he had completed the transformation he flew off into the west and has never been seen since."

Blyth didn't really know what to say, so he said nothing. There was a lengthy silence during which Kaito made an infusion rather more mundane than the one he had given Blyth earlier. He passed a cup to Blyth.

"You asked me about the infusion I gave you earlier," he began. "The effects are unpredictable. I sensed that you began to experience some rather unpleasant visions and I took the liberty of smoothing them away, but I can't do that if I am not there with you. It is also why I created an area which you could not easily leave: to keep you safe if the experiment went wrong. The longer-term effects are equally difficult to predict for certain but, in my limited experience, the sparing use of that drink can help to alleviate the worst of the Gods' curse. By opening up the channels of communication with the Gods you are able to gain some power over their curse. But you must resist the temptation to indulge too frequently in such experiments. Opening up those channels may lead you to make the journey all the way to the land of the Gods and never return."

Blyth's face gave away the fleeting thought that he would not object too strongly to such an outcome. Kaito did not directly read his thoughts but he had a good idea what had crossed Blyth's mind.

"Perhaps, if not for the sake of Blodwyth and Kallon, then for my sake? You might at least do me the kindness of allowing me to go there before you, since it seems neither my son nor your father had the courtesy to do so?"

Blyth looked down at the floor and then up to meet Kaito's eyes directly, an effort which Kaito knew cost him dearly.

"I promise at least to outlive you, if the Gods should will it."

"Thank you. I can ask no more. There is another matter, however."

Blyth's inquisitive look was enough for Kaito to continue.

"We spoke at length about the different beliefs about the Gods that are held by different tribes. I told you about those in the lands of the rising sun, far beyond Rome, who believe that life moves in a circle, just as the year begins with Samhain and the dark of winter and cycles through Imbolc and the new green of spring, Beltane and the heat of summer, and the harvest at Lughnasadh, before it comes back round to another year."

Blyth nodded, "Samsāra."

Kaito smiled and went on, "So, too, they believe that when a life ends, it begins anew in a new body."

"Punarbharva."

"Exactly; and do you remember also that I told you they believe the creature whose form you take on next is dependent on how well you have served the Gods?"

Blyth looked downcast.

"If their beliefs turn out to be correct, then your actions on the journey in search of Blodwyth set you backwards some considerable way. Either way, you would do well to put some effort into helping others and doing no harm as much as you can, if only because it is the right thing to do."

"Have I not done the right thing here this past year? Have I not taken good care of Blodwyth and my son, worked hard to help Biarni and Biarnafa with their farm?"

"Are you addressing me or the Gods?" Kaito asked simply, and Blyth deflated, knowing that his protestations meant nothing unless the Gods believed him and, deep down, he knew he could have done better. At that moment he made a mental promise to himself that he would do so.

Epilogue

Gwenn stood on the slope overlooking the town of Brigantio, the sun reflecting off the surface of the lake as it lowered in the western sky. She hoped somehow to see Glaessa from a distance and surprise her.

"Gwenn?" The voice came from close behind her.

She turned and caught sight of Glaessa's radiant face and copper hair reflecting the amber sunlight. They walked together in comfortable silence towards the town and Gwenn had never felt safer with the vast bulk of the greatest mountain range in the world between her and the hated Romani. Here was a land that would never be dominated by Rome, where she could live in peace for the rest of her life.

Notes

When I first began this series, I never imagined how fraught it could get writing a fantasy story set in a real historical setting. I decided that I would not change any known aspect of history, the winners and losers would be the same, the great people and the major events would all be preserved, but my stories would follow an undercurrent of unwritten events.

I wanted to slot a world of magic in between the real world of iron-age Celts and the Roman republic which means that magic users could not be too excessively powerful, or they could destroy whole armies with a wave of their hand. Instead, the druids, even the most powerful of them, must draw on enormous energy to cast spells, and this leaves them drained for some time.

When it comes to sticking to history, I have tried hard and spent far more hours researching than writing. In the course of writing this book and the ones before it, I have learned a lot more than you will from reading them, and that's fine. They are not supposed to be history books and you should not use them as source material.

In writing a book set in a historical setting there are different problems depending on how well recorded the history of the period is.

In the case of the Roman Republic, there is a great deal of well documented information, both about events and about every aspect of society. The problem with this is that I am not a professional academic historian and despite all my research I can never be as expert on the subject as such a person. In fact, even as an author, I am still a complete novice compared with the likes of Ruth Downie, Caroline Lawrence, or Colleen McCullough all of whom have immersed themselves fully in the subject in ways I can only dream of.

Then there are historical situations like iron-age Britain, and to some extent Alexandria at the time of this novel. Here we have far less detailed information, and a lack of reliable written records, especially contemporary written records. Much is lost in the mists of time, and so it might seem safe to make things up. I have indeed made a lot up, while always trying to keep to what is probable, or at least possible, but that doesn't mean I haven't sometimes made errors which more learned historians wouldn't be appalled by. I apologise to them and trust that the reader will not use my books to settle any arguments in history lessons.

Lastly there are the really undocumented situations. I could scarcely find anything at all about the people who lived in Scotland at that time, so I took my cue from the Ptolemy's Geography which was produced around 150CE. Ptolemy recorded several tribe names which may have been accurate or not. The people we call the Picts may have been descended from these tribes and so I described some of their clothing as having Pictish symbols on them. But the name Pict comes from Latin for "painted" and may not have had any relation to their own name for themselves. The types of buildings are better known since they leave archaeological records, but even these are incomplete. I had similar problems finding out about Scandinavia at that time. I had to assume a sort of proto-Viking Germanic tribal culture, with close trading and cross-cultural links with the Celts, Belgae (who may or may not have been Celtic) and of course the people of what is now Scotland.

The next book involves a long journey to the source of the Nile and into the Congolese rainforest. I know there were people there but as to their culture, language, or frankly anything about them, there seems to be almost nothing. This book took me an enormous amount of time to write because I was worried about getting too much wrong. The next may take even longer. For that reason, I tried hard to give this one a settled ending.

Glossary

- **Achilleos** – Yarrow plants of the genus Achillea have certain blood clotting properties and there is a legend that Achilles soldiers used them to stem bleeding from wounds. **kwaitarkos**

- **Auctoritas** – This is the root of the modern English word "authority", but it means more than that. Auctoritas was a measure of the social standing and political credibility of an important Roman.

- **Bulla** – The bulla was an amulet worn by Roman boys as a symbol of their status. On coming of age usually at about 16, they would remove the bulla as part of a manhood ceremony.

- **Calligae** – The boots, or more descriptively heavy-duty sandals, worn by legionaries. They had nails in the soles to make them more hardwearing. The name of the Roman Emperor Calligula means "little boots".

- **Campania** – a region of Italia both in Roman times and to this day. The largest city is Naples (Neapolis in Roman times). Other cities include Capua and Pompeii.

- **Capua** – The city of Capua was founded by the Etruscans and was home to the gladiator school from which Spartacus and a number of other gladiators escaped, thus precipitating the third servile wars (slave revolt).

- **Chiton** – (hard "ch" like in "chaos" or "charisma" or if you want to be really authentic, more like in the Scottish "loch") A fairly simple form of tunic typically associated with the Greeks and therefore more or less standard throughout the Hellenic world.

- **Cisalpine Gaul** – The Romans referred to that part of Gaul on the Italian side of the alps as Gallia Cisalpina. The rest of Gaul on the far side was transalpina.

- **Cohort** – A division of a legion. At the time of this book there were ten cohorts in a legion. The first cohort consisted of 800 mean while the remaining nine had 480 men each. So the total men in a legion was 5,120

- **Consuls** – In the Roman Republic, two consuls were elected each year to rule jointly. Normally they could only be consul for one year although in previous years first Marius, and then Sulla had remained in power for many years. Because there were almost always different consuls each year, the years were named after them. So 72 BCE in our calendar was the year of Publicola and Clodianus.

- **Contubernium** – This is the smallest unit in the Roman army, consisting of ten men who shared a tent. The equivalent of a squad in the modern army.

- **Coup de grâce** – literally blow of mercy, is a quick, and relatively kind, death delivered to someone who is already injured beyond hope of medical aid and in great pain.

- **Crucified** – just for the removal of all doubt, crucifixion was (and rather more tragically still is, in certain circumstances and places) very much a real thing, although the most famous depiction of the process, that of Jesus of Nazareth, is not necessarily strictly historically accurate. There is a great deal of furious debate on the methods employed and just how long the agony might have been drawn out. It is highly probable that there was no one method used, and it could have different results depending on that. In every case is was an extremely degrading and painful way to die.

- **Darruwen** – Darruwen was a village mage at Ba-Dun in "Children of the Wise Oak" who took a dislike to Trethiwr, seeing him as a threat to his own power over the chief.

- **Days (Celtic)** – The Celts believed that, in the beginning, the darkness was created before the light. And therefore each day began and ended at sunset, not sunrise. Each year also began at the beginning of winter at the end of our October. Even well into the late middle ages, the new day began at sunset and it is the reason why some festivals make a big thing about the evening before the day, Hallowe'en being the Celtic new year of Samhain (pronounced Sa'ween).

- **Decanus** – This was the legionary in charge of the contubernium of ten men. So roughly equivalent to a corporal in the modern army.

- **Deceangli** – A Celtic tribe located roughly in North Wales.

- **Deru-Weido-Maywr** – The name Deru-Weido was a back-creation of a name for the druids which came from ancient proto-Indo-European, and proto-Celtic languages and roughly translates as "Wise Oak". I chose it because it also sounded a bit like "Druid" and while I make no claim for it as being a real historical name it has a ring of truth to it. The word "maywr" is cognate with the Welsh word "mawr" and English "major" and just means great. So Deru-Weido-Maywr just means "great wise oak", referring of course to Kaito who is the central core, indeed, the actual trunk of the druid tradition. What we really know for certain about the druids can be written on a postage stamp in magic marker, so I feel safe in making one of my characters the very first and most important of them all.

- **Deus Pater** – The great sky father God. The name is cognate with Jupiter (say it quickly and slur it) and also Zeus, Dis Fater, and several more traditional mythologies from across Eurasia.

- **Eiru** – an old name for Eire or Ireland.

- **Falernian** – Falernian wine was one of the most famous and expensive types of wine, made from grapes grown around Mount Falernus in the north of Campania. The most famous and finest of all these was the Opimian vintage of 121 BCE. This would have been the equivalent of a vintage Domaine Leroy, or Romanée-Conti, Grand Cru today.

- **Gallia Narbonensis** – The part of Gaul on the Mediterranean coast, roughly equivalent to Languedoc and Provence today. This part of Gaul was assimilated into the Roman empire during the 2nd C BCE in order to allow them to build a road, Via Domitia, to their provinces in Hispania (Spain). The main cities were the, centurics old, Greek colony of Massalia (Marseille) and the more recently founded Roman colony of Narbo (Narbonne).

- **Gallus** – In this context this is a Roman gladiator dressed in the style of a Gallic warrior although the word had several other meanings depending on context. At the time of the Spartacan revolt a gladiator was usually either a Gallus or a Thraex (Thracian) like Spartacus. They were not always actually of those races, but they were usually dressed as such. Earlier in the Republic, there were Samnite gladiators although they would have faded from prominence since the Samnites had been largely incorporated into the wider Republic by this time and, particularly in Campania, Samnite gladiators would have seemed in rather bad taste since Samnium bordered the region to the north-east.

- **Garum** – This is a strong-tasting sauce which most Romans used fairly liberally. The recipe is lost but appears to have been at least somewhat similar to how Worcestershire sauce is produced.

- **Gladius** – The standard Roman legionary sword which also gives its name to gladiators. It was short and had a sharp point designed for thrusting and stabbing, not for slashing. The Gauls of the period favoured a longer sword with a blunt tip used exclusively as a slashing weapon.

- **Greaves** – Leg armour, sometimes worn in pairs, but sometimes only on the leading leg. In some cases this may have had a more symbolic than strictly protective purpose.

- **Helleni** – The name for the Greek people in their language. Greek culture still dominated the Roman world and the Hellenic language would 'get you by' from Gaul to Egypt and from Hispania to Asia.

- **Homunculus** – A very small human or humanoid creature. In this case, Khemi is specifically a vervet monkey which would have been common enough in Ethiopia and Southern Sudan for specimens to be brought to Egypt by traders.

- **Insulae** – With a very high population density, Roman builders built what we would call blocks of flats, or apartment blocks. They stood out high above the sea of single or double storey villas surrounding them like islands. The Latin word for islands is insulae.

- **Italia** – The Latin (and indeed Italian) word for Italy.

- **Kwaitarkos** – See Achilleos.

- **Lanista** – An owner of gladiators and usually a gladiator school (ludo). He was considered of low status, but it was a lucrative business to be in, hiring out gladiators for games.
- **Latifundia** – Huge farms which were created by wealthy patricians who could afford to buy up land from those who had fallen on hard times or had their lands stripped from them during the period of Sulla's proscriptions. Certain individuals and families had all their property taken away from them for supporting Marius.
- **Legate** – A very senior rank in the Roman army. The legate was in command of an entire legion, subordinate only to the overall commanding general.
- **Legion** – obviously this is a huge subject and impossible to cover fully here. During the period of this book a typical Roman legion consisted of 5,120 men divided into ten cohorts, one of 800 men and the other nine of 480. The cohort was divided into 6 centuries of 80 men each (not 100) led by a centurion.

  In addition there were 640 mules and a large number of additional personnel including camp followers, and slaves bringing the total number up to as many as 11,000 people. When on the march, if facing hostile opposition, the legion would have to build a new temporary fortified camp at every overnight stop.

- **Ludus** – Latin word for game/sport/training. Plural ludi. So the gladiatorial games were called ludi, but also a gladiator school was a ludus.
- **Manumission** – The legal process of freeing a slave. Just saying "you're freed" would not be legally binding. The proper paperwork had to be done and witnessed, and sometimes money paid either by the slave (they were permitted to own property) or by the master.
- **Marius** – Gaius Marius was one of the greatest generals that Rome ever produced. He lived from 157BCE – 86BCE and among his achievements were the final destruction of the Germanic tribes of Cimbri and others who had previously inflicted some of the worst defeats on the Roman legions in history. He also reformed how the legions were recruited and constructed, making Rome a more effective military power.
- **Mater** – One of the oldest words in human communication is "mother". It is logical because it is such an important concept, but we also know it is very old because almost every word in every language is similar. Mater is Latin for mother, it's mutter in German and despite being fam in Welsh, I decided the Celts would probably be very similar to the Romans at the time.
- **Mentula** – Ah! Err, this is just a crude way of saying penis in Latin. There, I said it. Have fun!

- **Militia** – When you need an army but there isn't a legion nearby, or when you don't think the threat is serious as was the case at the start of the Spartacan revolt, you raise a militia of willing volunteers. Some would have been military veterans who still owned their own armour and weapons, others would have been young men or traders who felt it important to help out with a temporary threat. Obviously the militia sent against Spartacus expected to round the slaves up easily and were not expecting to be completely annihilated.

- **Musaeon** – This is the original museum, or Musaeum which takes its name from the nine muses of Greek mythology and was built

- **Novantae** – A (probably) Celtic tribe located in the Galloway region of Scotland. Little is known of them other than a reference from Ptolemy's geography from circa 150CE but there is archaeological evidence of continuous occupation from around 100BCE, so I took the liberty of assuming the tribal name had remained the same for this whole period.

- **Opimian** – See Falernian.

- **Palatine** – Rome was built on seven hills, named Aventine, Caelian, Capitoline, Esquiline, Palatine, Quirinal, and Viminal. Of these the most central was the Palatine hill on which later emperors built their palaces, and indeed is the root of the modern word palace.

- **Parthi** – The Parthian (a.k.a. the Arsacid) Empire, was the dominant power in the middle east at the time of this series. It covered an area approximately equivalent to Iran, Iraq, Afghanistan, Turkmenistan, Uzbekistan, Tajikistan, Azerbaijan, Armenia, and parts of China, Pakistan, Syria, and Turkey.

- **Pilum** – This was a Roman javelin with a long iron shank and sharp point attached to a wooden shaft. The shank would usually bend or break off on impact making it impossible to throw back with any effect.

- **Phalerae** – These were silver (or sometimes gold or bronze) discs worn by legionaries who had been awarded them for bravery in combat. The equivalent of medals.

- **Plebeian** – In early Roman society, people were either patrician or plebeian. The patrician class were somewhat equivalent to aristocracy in modern times. However, although plebeians were originally the common class, by the late Republic the real commoners were the slaves and non-citizens, while many plebeians held high office and wielded considerable power.

- **Praetor** – This was an official Roman position below the two Consuls. At the time of the story there were usually eight praetors who, like consuls, had functions ranging from administration and judicial to commanding legions.

- **Proscriptions** – Prior to the setting of this book the Roman republic went through a long period of upheaval largely driven by a feud between two powerful politician/generals: Marius and Sulla. Marius became consul multiple times and used his power to weaken supporters of Sulla. When Sulla finally seized power he used his power even more brutally to destroy Marius and all his supporters. The proscriptions were lists of men whose property could be seized and their rights stripped. Many great and powerful men were reduced to penury or even killed at this time, while other men became fabulously wealthy by buying up this stolen land at ridiculously low prices.

- **Roundhouse** – The traditional form of dwelling in iron-age Britain and Gaul was a large circular house made from a timber frame (or more rarely stone) with a steep conical thatched roof. Further north in what is now Scotland, these houses were more likely to be built from stone, and were often quite complex structures on more than one floor, to allow the animals to be brought in from the cold and to withstand the worst winters.

- **Samhain** – Pronounced *"Sa-ween"* This is the Celtic New Year which took place at our Halloween. Like most strong pre-Christian festivals, e.g. Mayday (another Celtic one) or Easter and Christmas (not Celtic) this festival has been usurped and replaced by a Christianised version.

- **Scutum** – The classic Roman shield, a tall, curved, rectangle of wood with a heavy bronze boss and reinforcements. It gave good protection when used in tight formation and employing the gladius to stab, rather than slash, the enemy. The scutum was itself also a fearsome weapon, being used to push and thrust the enemy back, smashing into chests with the metal boss.
- **Senate** – The senate was one of the most important official bodies of the very complex political system of the Roman republic. Any attempt to summarise it adequately here would be counterproductive.

- **Shang-chi** – This can't be adequately explained here but I'll try. The game of xiangqi is similar to chess and is played widely in China to this day. Most historians accept that it grew either alongside or as a variant of chaturanga which is a precursor to modern day chess. However, there is another, less accepted version of events which claims the game was developed by general Han Xin in 203-204BCE. While historical evidence is lacking, I decided to accept that version, but I spelled the name more or less phonetically allowing for some mispronunciation due to mishearing and different linguistic forms. The game that Teague plays, which is also similar to chess and to xiangqi, is entirely my own conceit based on a firm belief that just because there isn't a shred of evidence for something doesn't mean it cannot have happened. If an intelligent Celtic traveller visited Persia, China, or India, which a few surely must, and they *didn't* come back with cultural traditions which they then adapted to their own culture, it would defy all reason and logic.

- **Sicilia** – (*pronounced Si-Kill-ia.*)* This is the Latin name for Sicily. (It is spelled the same in modern Italian, but they pronounce it Si-Chill-ia)
  N.B. All Latin Cs are hard. E.g. Caesar is pronounced Kaiser.

- **Talent** – Most readers will be familiar with the parable of the talents from the bible, but many will not be aware that a talent is actually a measure of weight, and not a set monetary value. A Roman talent was equal to 100 Librae which was equivalent to just over 32kg.
- **Taranis** – Taranis is a god of thunder (and presumably lightning otherwise what's the point?) in Celtic mythology. There are others, but he's the best known.
- **The halls of Lugh** – This one is really contentious, and I make no pretence that this is historically accurate. Lugh is one of the more important Celtic gods, but scholars can't agree on the details. I have taken his name to be cognate with light although there are valid arguments against this. I also place him as the chief "nice" god and although there are scholars who argue that the Celts did not have the same notion of a heavenly afterlife as later religions, I just flat out don't accept that. I am confident if we could travel back in time and speak to living iron-age Celts they would fervently tell you that those who served the gods well would spend their next life drinking and feasting with Lugh and all the best gods. Those who were cast out by the Druids or who did terrible things like wasting good boar would spend their next life in darkness and cold. (Or something like that. Do feel free to believe what you want because I am certain we will NEVER know)

- **Torc** – A circlet of metal with one side open to allow it to be placed around the neck or the wrists and worn as jewellery. Torcs could be of silver, or gold, but also of bronze, copper, or iron. They could be used as currency if needed but wearing valuable torcs was also a symbol of status in society.

- **Trethiwr** – In the first book in the series, Trethiwr is the father of Blyth, Teague, Abbon, and Elarch, and the life partner of Epona, their mother. He featured for only a few chapters in the book, coming back from travelling in Egypt and then being brutally killed in a seemingly inexplicable set of circumstances which, frankly, wasn't explained very well until this book.

- **Tribune** – This is an official Roman title with several different types. There were ten tribunes of the plebs (see plebeian) who acted as a check on the authority of the senate. Then there were a number of military tribunes who were in charge of a part of the army and acted as close assistants to the general.

- **Urien** – The Celtic chief of the village of Ba-Dun where Blyth, Teague, Abbon, and Elarch all grew up. Their father was murdered by the mage who was then struck by lightning in a moment of perfect karma, and there has been degree of ill feeling between Urien and Trethiwr's family ever since. In fact, arguably, it predates even those events.

- **Woad** – Woad is a dark blue dye derived from *Isatis tinctoria*. It doesn't grow in colder climates like Scotland but manages ok in southern England. Celts used it as a fabric dye.
  N.B. Probably not a tattoo ink: Julius Caesar stated, unequivocally, that they used woad to tattoo themselves. However, woad does not 'fix' and causes agonising burning when applied under the skin. Some Celts may well have used some form of tattooing or blue coloured face-paints, but I suspect that Caesar either misunderstood what they told him it was, or they were pulling his leg, hoping he might try to get a woad tattoo and end up screaming in agony. Alternatively woad may have been added in small quantities to a mixture of other ingredients such as rust, copper oxides, and ash, mixed into strong alcohol. Whatever they did use will almost certainly never be known and PLEASE do not try to experiment with these things yourself.

Blue Poppy Publishing

If you have enjoyed this book, we sincerely hope you can find time to write a review on Amazon and/or Goodreads.

Blue Poppy was set up to publish the first in the Wise Oak series by Oliver J. Tooley and has since gone on to publish around a dozen other authors and many more titles.

Predominantly focussed on books by authors from Devon, England, or books which are set in the South West of England, where we are based. You can discover more about other Blue Poppy books at our website www.bluepoppypublishing.co.uk

Printed in Great Britain
by Amazon